Murder's Long Memory

by the same author

TOO CLEVER BY HALF
DEAD CLEVER
DEATH TRICK
RELATIVELY DANGEROUS
ALMOST MURDER
LAYERS OF DECEIT
THREE AND ONE MAKE FIVE
DEADLY PETARD
UNSEEMLY END
JUST DESERTS
MURDERS BEGETS MURDER
TROUBLED DEATHS
TWO-FACED DEATH
MISTAKENLY IN MALLORCA
DEAD MAN'S BLUFF
A TRAITOR'S CRIME
A DEADLY MARRIAGE
DEATH IN THE COVERTS
DEAD AGAINST THE LAWYERS
AN EMBARRASSING DEATH
THE BENEFITS OF DEATH
EXHIBIT No. THIRTEEN
EVIDENCE OF THE ACCUSED

RODERIC JEFFRIES

Murder's Long Memory

An Inspector Alvarez novel

St. Martin's Press
New York

Library of Congress Cataloging-in-Publication Data

Jeffries, Roderic
   Murder's long memory / Roderic Jeffries.
     p.   cm.
   ISBN 0-312-07039-X
   I. Title.
 PR6060.E43M8   1992
 823'.914—dc20   91-38237
                                                    CIP

First published in Great Britain by William Collins Sons & Company Limited.

First U.S. Edition: April 1992
10 9 8 7 6 5 4 3 2 1

Murder's Long Memory

CHAPTER 1

Call no man accursed until he dies, he is at worst unfortunate. Back in January, Madge had left him on a Monday, in order to move in with Aubrey, who had been his best friend; it was very sad to lose a best friend. On Wednesday he had learned that his 'Nubian in Love' had failed to win the first prize of five thousand guineas; 'Consumption in Red'—a collection of old tin cans and chicken bones painted red—had been declared a winner. And on Saturday his mother had died unexpectedly, leaving him bewildered that at the age of fifty he could still feel so great a sense of loss.

Steven Armitage looked around the sitting-room of the small country cottage in which his mother had lived for the past forty-five years. Nothing had yet been touched and it was all too easy to expect her to walk in and ask him if he'd like some coffee, knowing full well that he'd prefer a stiff whisky. On the top shelf to the right of the inglenook fireplace were three framed photographs. The one on the left was of his father, in naval uniform. Strange to think that he had never known the man who'd sired him. The centre one had been taken on his mother's wedding day; she had never been beautiful, but this photograph captured both her highly developed sense of fun and of loyalty. He occupied the right-hand one, at the age of four and looking angelic—she'd often said that that proved the camera always lied; a couple of minutes after the photo had been taken he had caused havoc.

There was a knock and he went into the hall and across to the front door.

'Good afternoon, Mr Armitage. I do hope I'm not too late, but there was rather a lot of traffic.'

'You're on time. I arrived early.'

'Yes, of course. Memories.'

Shankley, of Brade and Elliott, was probably a loving, caring husband and father, but Armitage did not like him.

'A very sad time,' said Shankley solemnly.

'Yes, it is,' replied Armitage curtly; grief was an emotion he was not prepared to share with the other. 'Shall we go through?'

In the sitting-room, Shankley sat on one of the armchairs and rested the briefcase on his knees. 'I always feel that this is a time when—'

'A drink's a good idea. So what will you have?'

Shankley showed neither resentment at the brusque manner in which he'd been cut short, nor any sense of disapproval at Armitage's apparent lack of emotional reaction to his mother's death. 'A sherry, please, if you have one.'

Armitage went over to the small cupboard in the far corner, to the right of a well-filled bookcase. There were several bottles inside. His mother had always enjoyed alcohol and unlike so many women had never made any bones about the fact, but she'd never had more than two drinks, not even on his wedding day. Perhaps she'd known more than he had. 'Sweet or dry?'

'Dry, if I may.'

He poured out a copita of La Ina and then a double whisky for himself. Both Madge and his mother had repeatedly admonished him over his heavy drinking; Madge illtemperedly, his mother sadly. 'D'you smoke?' he asked, as he handed over the glass of sherry.

'No, thanks. I gave it up several years ago.'

He sat in the second armchair and lit a cheroot. 'So how far have we got?'

Shankley put the glass down on the piecrust table to his right. He opened the briefcase and brought out a folder, laid the briefcase flat on his knees and set the folder down on this. 'Everything's progressing smoothly and there shouldn't be any unusual delay in obtaining probate. The valuations have all been accepted.' He opened the folder and shuffled through papers until he found the one he wanted. 'As regards the furniture, there's one piece of consequence. The desk in the first bedroom is valued at five thousand pounds and the valuer confided in me that it could well fetch considerably more. He also said that if you decided to sell, you might well consider sending it up to one of the major London auction houses.'

'I didn't realize it was that good.'

'The house has been valued at two hundred thousand pounds. Naturally, the amount it fetches, should you decide to sell, will depend on the current state of the market; but period cottages are maintaining their value even at this time of difficulty in the property market . . . I have prepared a copy of all the figures, which you will no doubt wish to have.' He stood, his movements slightly clumsy, and leaned forward to hand across two sheets of paper stapled together.

Armitage studied the figures and was surprised at the total. It seemed he was going to inherit considerably more than he had imagined. He was glad that Madge had left him before he had had any idea of the extent of his coming good fortune.

'Do you think you will sell the house, Mr Armitage?'

'I haven't thought about it.'

'No, of course not; it's far too early. But when you do and should you decide to sell, might I suggest you employ the firm which has made the valuation? I can thoroughly recommend them and they'll certainly obtain the best possible price.'

'I'll remember that.'

'Spring is the best time to put a property on the market; winter is to be avoided if at all possible. Grey skies make for grey prices.'

'I'll remember that as well.'

'These little points can make a difference of several thousands of pounds,' said Shankley defensively.

'I'm sure they can,' said Armitage, trying to sound grateful.

Shankley coughed. 'There is one point which we should discuss—if that's all right with you?'

'Sure.'

'It concerns your mother's income at the time she died. I believe you told me that she had only her two pensions and the income from the capital in her building society account.'

'That's right.'

'You are quite certain of that?'

'Yes.'

'Please don't misunderstand me, I'm not suggesting that you are trying to hide anything. All I am saying is that . . . Well, to be perfectly frank, old ladies can become so secretive about money that even their own children don't know all the sources of their income. And you will understand that if the probate officer begins to question the figures, even though the valuations have been accepted, we may have to be more precise. This can be something of an embarrassment. It might be held, for instance, that the desk should be declared at the higher rather than the lower figure of its value range.'

'My mother had no secret cache of gold.'

'The problem is the size of her naval widow's pension.'

'Why?'

'As I understand it, when your father died he was a lieutenant?'

'That's right.'

'The pension paid to the widow of a naval lieutenant killed during the last war is considerably less than she declared each year to the tax authorities.'

'It is?' he said, surprised.

'You didn't know this?'

'She handled all her own financial affairs.' She had often told him that he understood as much about money as a cherub did about hell.

'Then perhaps this is a point which is best left to rest in the hopes that the problem may not be raised.'

Shankley obviously reckoned there was something finan-
cially fishy going on, Armitage thought. Solicitors were like
policemen, they couldn't really believe in the existence of
innocence. He drained his glass, stood. 'Drink up and I'll
get the other half.'

'Not for me, thanks. I never have more than one.'

He looked a one-drink man. Armitage crossed to the
drinks cupboard and poured himself another double Scotch.

He stood in his mother's bedroom and through the leaded
window watched Shankley drive away in a Rover. He
turned. His mother had died in bed, during the night, and
on her face in the morning there had been an expression of
calm satisfaction. He had wept no tears at the time, nor
were any threatening now, yet the sense of loss was increas-
ing rather than diminishing. The past had been torn away
and he now had nowhere to run to for succour. Not, ironically, that he had ever run to her. She had taught him that
one lived with one's mistakes. But the disappearance of a
refuge he would never have used left him uneasy, even
afraid . . .

The room was the smallest of the three bedrooms, but
she had chosen it because it caught the morning sun. It
contained a single bed, a bedside table, a chest-of-drawers,
a dressing-table, a chair with needlework seat, an Indian
carpet which his father had bought in Bombay, the desk
which had aroused Shankley's enthusiasm, and a framed
print of a Yorkshire scene, just below Long Preston. Opposite the bed was a cupboard, made by boxing-in the space
around the massive chimney. It was filled with clothes. He'd
offered them to the Red Cross, an organization for the relief
of distressed gentlefolk, and the daily, but all had refused
them; it seemed that in these days second-hand clothes were
viewed with scorn even by those in need—or perhaps an
old woman's clothes became too impregnated with age even
for charity.

He went over to the desk. On the narrow top was a second

photograph of his father in open shirt and creased flannels, laughing, curly hair windswept, with a pebble beach and frisky sea behind him. He and his father were totally dissimilar in appearance. His mother, whose sense of humour had often offended the pompous, had sometimes said that he was so different in all respects that perhaps he was a changeling. Had this levity concealed a regret that he was not more like his father both in character and appearance?

He opened the curved top of the desk which, when the two supports were slid out, provided a working surface. At the back were four pigeonholes and six drawers, three on either side. Previously, he'd cleared the pigeonholes, but not the drawers. They contained a number of mementoes and the usual odds and ends of an inveterate letter-writer. He put the mementoes on one side, together with a couple of BB pencils, and tipped everything else into a waste-paper bin. He imagined someone clearing up after his own death. Into the rubbish bin with 'Nubian in Love' . . .

He remembered that there was a secret drawer, but not its exact location. It took him several minutes to discover that it had to be at the back of the bottom right-hand drawer; several more, equally frustrating, to learn how to release the spring catch of the false back. Inside were two envelopes. He opened the first. It contained a block of four penny blacks. He stared at them, wondering where they could have come from since his mother had never shown the slightest interest in collecting stamps and then decided that the only point of any importance was that the so-honest Shankley knew nothing about them. The second envelope was addressed to Mrs G. Lance, c/o Mrs R. Hammer, 75A Hopecroft Rd, Hanwell, London, W7. The stamp was Portuguese and the postmark Lisbon, dated an unreadable day in October 1942. The handwriting was his father's. He brought out the letter inside. It began, 'Darling Guinevere . . . '; it was signed, 'all my love, Merlin.' It spoke of missing her more than he had dreamed possible, a loss which had become still more acute when he had returned to their magical picnic spot and had looked down on the fishing village of Exchaux and the surrounding orange and almond groves and had remembered how intensely happy they'd been . . . And what but remembered love could have produced Pedro the Iceman, leading his donkey with the straw-lined panniers on either side. Pedro had remembered him and had asked how the lovely lady was . . .

His father's name had been Peregrine and his mother's had been Charlotte. This was a love-letter to another woman. His father, whose memory he had been taught to revere, had been an adulterer. It sickened him to know that his mother had had to live with the knowledge that she had been betrayed. One's parent was not allowed the luxury of having the same weaknesses as oneself . . .

And then he began to wonder why his mother had kept the letter. And the only reason he could conceive was that she had wanted to keep the pain alive. It was a side of her character that he could not even have guessed at; especially since that made her such a hypocrite for having always praised his father as a man of absolute honour. Or had she hoped against hope that he would try to emulate the false picture rather than imitate the true one?

He wished to God he'd never found and read the letter. He replaced it in the secret compartment of the desk, without any definite reason for doing so, then went downstairs where he poured himself a third, and even stronger, whisky.

CHAPTER 2

On the Monday that Madge had left him, she had worked herself up into a hysterical rage because that had been the only way in which she could justify her actions to herself— an uncertain woman, she was forever troubled that others would consider her actions unjustified or ill-bred. During her rage, she had shouted that she was leaving him because she could no longer stand living in a pigsty. Dandor Cottage was far from that, but in comparison with the Georgian house in which Aubrey lived, it did lack style. It lay at the end of a gloomy, no-throughway lane and it had been built just under two hundred years before to what had clearly been a very tight budget. Since then, its fortunes had not improved. The old peg-tiles had, where necessary, been replaced by modern tiles of a particularly objectionable red so that the roof looked to be suffering from eczema; the windows were small and one of Madge's friends had compared them to evil eyes; the room downstairs smelled of damp. But the rent was low and the adjoining barn was in surprisingly good repair so that it made an excellent studio.

He sat in the more comfortable of the easy chairs in the small, low-ceilinged sitting-room and wondered if it were time to switch on the television? He realized that since Madge wasn't at home, there was no need to watch the news if he didn't want to and right then he didn't give a damn if the world was in terminal chaos. He realized something more. He could pour himself as many drinks as he liked without once being told that he was always ready to fund his own vices, but never to buy her any decent clothes . . .

There was just enough whisky in the bottle to provide a respectable drink. He returned to the sitting-room, then lit his fifth cheroot of the day—as a man of property, he could now afford luxuries. He blew out a cloud of smoke. What to do? Move into the cottage or sell it, invest the capital and enjoy an unearned income? Sculptors with an income were invariably seen to be more talented than those without. Gallery-owners welcomed those who were willing to defray part or all of the expenses of their exhibitions; the buying public would turn up to a champagne reception because, being by definition wealthy, they could never resist anything that was free; and every art critic alive divined quality in the work of a sculptor who had just had a case of Mouton Rothschild delivered to his door. Success once initiated, gathered its own and ever-increasing momentum . . .

He needed another drink, but the whisky bottle was empty. Wasn't there another hidden in the barn? Regretfully, he could remember emptying that two days ago. One of the last insults Madge had hurled at him had been that he'd become an alcoholic. She'd never been able to understand that there were times when an artist had to dull the pain of the artistic frustration within him.

He smoked and considered himself and didn't particularly like what he saw. A man who was enjoying a sneaking sense of gratification over the fact that he'd discovered his father had feet of clay; it was so much easier to measure oneself against a fallen idol. But what a way to gain one's gratification!

He suddenly stood and went through to the larder, which was beyond and outside the kitchen. Memory proved to be correct. There was a half-full bottle of Dubonnet. Madge had taken to drinking that the day after she'd read that it was the favourite tipple of one of the Royals. If a Royal had developed a taste for kava, she'd have drunk that.

An hour later, having discovered that whisky and Dubonnet were more potent in their whole than in their separate parts, he made his unsteady way up the stairs to the bedroom. As he stood in the doorway and stared blearily at the two single beds, he wondered if she'd demanded a single one in Aubrey's mansion or had so surrendered to passion as to agree to a double one?

He changed into pyjamas, climbed into bed. The world began to move and he closed his eyes. For no reason that seemed logical, it occurred to him that both Merlin and Peregrine were falcons. He slipped away into a dunken slumber.

When in Korinjora's company, he forgot that she was less than half his age, that there were threads of grey both in his hair and his beard, that the lines on his face were becoming deeper, that his facial skin was roughening, and that while his hands could have spanned her waist, her hands would have been lost around his . . .

She had been born in a village in Northern Sudan whose name was one he could neither remember nor, if reminded, pronounce. Her parents had come to England when she was in the cradle and she had lived in Torrington since then. She was tall, lithe, and strikingly, erotically attractive. She would even have evoked sexual fantasies in St Simeon as he sat high up on his pole. But in her tribe a woman went to her bridal bed a virgin or she shamed herself so seriously that only her death could restore honour to her family.

She loved to display her smooth perfection, seeing no cause for shame in nudity. She posed with taunting, tantalizing sensuality. It was this quality of offering what she would never give which had made 'Nubian in Love' so outstanding a sculpture. Outstanding, that was, to all but the purblind, ignorant judges.

'You're very silent this morning,' she said. She spoke idiomatic English with a lilt and an occasional change of rhythm that could add spice to the most ordinary of sentences. 'Are you angry with me?'

He was sculpting a bust and so there had been no need for her to strip, but she had ignored him when he'd told her this and she was naked. 'Have I cause to be?'

'Men become angry for very strange reasons.' She reached up to scratch her right breast.

'Keep still.'

'I have a tickle. If I can't scratch it, you will have to.'

'Haven't the time.' He used his thumb to ease the swell of a curve.

'I think you hate me,' she said sadly. This was a game with endless variations that was always played to the same rules.

'Think what you like.'

'Perhaps you would prefer me to be a boy? I have a friend who is very beautiful and he would come here. In my tribe, boys are not like girls.'

'How original!'

She laughed, white teeth flashing. 'Boys do not have to go to their wedding beds as virgins. Shall I ask him to come here and then you can be happy instead of a bear with a sore head?'

'You'll get a sore arse if he does.'

She laughed again. She enjoyed crudity.

He stepped back and regarded the bust, still in very rough form. 'All right, let's break for coffee.'

She came across and stood close to him. 'Do my tits really look like that?'

'They won't come right,' he replied angrily. He'd known without her questioning the work that everything done that morning had been a waste of time. There were days when his fingers were traitors. He turned, crossed to the far side of the beamed barn where there was a cold-water tap, a one-burner gas ring, and a worm-eaten cupboard. He brought out a battered kettle, filled this with water, put it on the ring and lit the gas. 'D'you want a smoke?'

'Yes, massa.' She loved playing a part. Often, she was a slave and he was her owner, entitled to do with her as he wanted.

He went over to his coat hanging on the back of a battered kitchen chair, and brought out of the pocket a pack in which were two cheroots. She took one, rolled it between her fingers and put it in her mouth; movements to which she gave an unmistakable connotation. 'You want to give me fire, massa?'

'Light your own.' He threw a box of matches across. He wondered if she knew how fiercely his fires of desire burned at times, realized that that was a naïve question. Yet if he ever allowed those fires to burn too fiercely, she would then regard him with a measure of contempt. She respected strength.

She lit the cheroot. 'Steven . . .' She paused, as she handed back the matches. 'Is something wrong?' With mercurial speed, her manner had changed and now she was completely serious.

'Why d'you ask?'

'Because you aren't yourself.'

'I had a thick night.'

'Because she's left you to go off with that bastard?' She never referred to Madge by name. Perhaps she knew that Madge had always called her 'that savage'.

'No.'

'What then?'

'There's no firm reason.'

'Don't be silly, man. There's something bugging you hard.

'If there is, it's none of your business.'

'We have a saying. To share is to halve.'

'That applies only to missionaries.'

She came forward and placed a hand on his arm. 'I am your friend. Tell me.'

They would have presented an unusual picture to an outsider—a naked black girl pleading to a middle-aged white man. Yet it was one of the most genuine offers of help that he had ever received. He cleared his throat. It was not going to be easy, because emotionally he was a very secretive man. 'I learned something yesterday which hurt.'

The kettle began to boil. He switched off the gas, opened the cupboard again and produced two mugs, a tin of instant coffee, a bowl of sugar, and a canteen teaspoon. He made the coffee, passed one mug across. 'Let's sit.'

There was an old chaise-longue, used when he wanted a reclining figure, and the kitchen chair. She settled on the chaise-longue. It had not occurred to her to slip on the old woollen dressing-gown that was hanging on a wall, used by models less proud of their nakedness than she, and he was able to watch the play of her muscles.

She drank, tipped ash on to the floor. 'What has hurt you so badly?'

He told her, at first haltingly, then more fluently.

'How did your father die?'

'He was shot by the Germans in France as a spy. After the war he was posthumously awarded the George Medal.'

'So he was a great hero?'

'As were hundreds of others.'

'Why add that? Their bravery cannot diminish his.'

'I didn't mean it like that. I was just . . .' He stopped.

'Just being very British and denigrating what you most admire. Your mother told you again and again that he was a hero so you have always looked up to him as a very great man; yet now you are prepared to think him a no-good man simply because he had another woman?'

'Not no-good; of course not . . . But not the knight in shining armour because of what he did to my mother.'

'For my people, there is no such thing as adultery. After marriage, women as well as men can enjoy themselves as they wish. If a man sleeps with a hundred women, that does not make him any less the man he was.'

'It's different for someone who's believed all his life that his father possessed only good qualities and then suddenly discovers that maybe he lacked the most important.'

'Was your mother a fool?'

'She'd a mind as sharp as a razor right up to the day of her death.'

'Was she dishonest morally?'

'As honest as anyone could be.'

'Then why should she have lied to you?'

'I suppose, to protect me from the truth.'

'A clever person doesn't try to do that because she knows the truth always eventually comes to the surface. So was she vindictive?'

'I've often told her that she was far too forgiving for a world in which forgiveness is usually seen as weakness.'

'Was she a mental masochist?'

'What the hell sort of a question is that supposed to be?'

'We have a saying. To cure a snake bite, it is necessary to cut the flesh.'

'Your tribe has more sayings than an Irish comedian . . .

My mother was not a mental masochist—whatever that is—and to satisfy your curiosity, neither did she go in for sadism. She was just a woman with rather higher standards than most.'

'Then why did she keep the letter for nearly fifty years?'

'If I knew the answer to that, I wouldn't be kicking my mind around so hard.'

'Why are you so certain it was a love-letter?'

'Because, back in those days, people showed more constraint than now and didn't go into passionate fantasies when they were just pen pals.'

'Then something has to be wrong.'

'Something is wrong but, goddamnit, what? Mother always said that Father was in France for several weeks before he was caught; yet according to this letter, he was in Portugal just three weeks before then. And . . .'

'And what?'

'And why Merlin?'

'Who is Merlin?'

'I told you, that's how Father signed himself in the letter. His christian name was Peregrine. Both peregrine and merlin are falcons.'

'A man . . .' She stopped.

'Don't bother to tell me that a married man who's writing to another woman often uses a false name to hide his identity. I know that. But I'm not certain it's that simple. Merlin was at the court of King Arthur, whose wife was Guinevere.'

'You are saying that it is a simple code?'

'My mother loved the Arthurian legends. But why in hell would my father write to my mother in any sort of a code?'

'Yet if he did, it would explain why she'd kept the letter all these years, wouldn't it?'

'The happy ending. You women always yearn for the sentimental finale.'

'Why shouldn't we want life to be nice? . . . You are going to find out the truth about this letter?'

'After fifty years?'

'Don't be so defeatist.'

'Then tell me why I should? By introducing King Arthur, I've provided myself with the means to believe the best, not the worst.'

'So you too want the happy ending?'

'Can't you bloody well keep quiet for ten seconds? . . . Suppose I manage to find out the truth and discover that my Arthurian escape was false and this letter was written to another woman? Then I can't fool myself into believing what I want to.'

'My tribe has a saying.'

'Your tribe suffers from verbal diarrhoea.'

'Better to face the devil, however ugly he is, than to risk his coming up from behind . . . You must try to find out the truth, so that you know. You are a smart man and you understand the real person behind the mask. Had your mother been the kind of person to keep that letter in order to enjoy the pain it gave her, you would have known that she was not truly a wonderful woman. So please, please, find out the truth so that you can no longer have any secret doubts.' She came off the chaise-longue to stand immediately in front of him, her expression both command-ing and beseeching, her muscles tensed as if she were about to explode into violent physical action.

He wished he had the power to carve her as he now saw her; but he doubted whether even Michelangelo could have have succeeded in doing that.

CHAPTER 3

On a grey, overcast, drizzling day in one of London's less salubrious suburbs, it became very difficult to believe that there was the slightest logic to his quest. He queued inside the post office until it was his turn to move forward and then he crossed to the Inquiries counter. The woman behind this soon proved to be of a far more helpful disposition than her appearance had suggested.

'I've never heard of Hopecroft Road. I suppose you are sure that it's here and not in West Ealing or even Southall?'

'The address is definitely Hanwell, West Seven.'

'Then I'll have a look in the books and see.'

She was gone a short while. When she returned, she said: 'I'm sorry, but there is no Hopecroft Road in Hanwell. And just in case, I checked the rest of London and there isn't one anywhere else; just a Hopetown and a Hopewell. D'you think that it could be one of those in spite of the West Seven?'

'Not really.'

'No, I suppose not . . . Look, why don't you get back on to whoever gave you the address and check it out?'

He smiled briefly. 'I'm afraid that that's not possible. The letter was written almost fifty years ago and both the writer and the person to whom it was written are dead.'

She looked curiously at him, wondering why he should be pursuing the matter after so long a time. 'Of course, names do alter and maybe that's what's happened. We had a Joseph Pierce Street until the poor man did something that upset the council and then the name was suddenly changed.'

'How could I find out if there was a Hopecroft Road back in the 'forties?'

'I suppose you could go through the old street directories. I'd do that for you, but we only keep them here for ten years back. And I can't say offhand where you could look at the really old ones . . . Your best bet might be to have a word with old Charlie Brane. He worked on deliveries for years and years and he might know if there was once a Hopecroft Road.'

'Where can I find him?'

'His address will be in the pensions book. Hang on and I'll look it up for you.'

She was away for nearly five minutes and when she returned she handed him a slip of paper on which she'd written the address. He thanked her and left, conscious of the hostile looks from people in the queue who resented the length of time he'd occupied the counter.

His Metro was parked forty yards down the road. It started on the first turn of the key. It might look like a refugee from a breaker's yard, but mechanically it was in good shape. He went up Church Road and Greenford Avenue, turned off into a maze of small, short roads which, after one false run, brought him to Glenmorrie Avenue. As he climbed out of the car, he wondered who had decided on so inappropriate a name? The glens were a million miles away from this ugly suburban backwater.

A middle-aged, dumpy woman answered the door. Her initial attitude was hostile, perhaps because of his beard she judged him to be a religious nut, but as soon as he explained the reason for his visit, she became friendly. 'Dad's in the front room, watching the telly. Doesn't do much else these days. Still, it keeps him quiet. And that's something, with him and the boys arguing over everything.'

Her words built up in his mind the picture of an old and partially senile man whose mumblings and physical infirmities provoked scorn and resentment from his grandchildren. Reality provided a sprightly cock robin of a man whose only infirmity was an overloose tongue. It was some time before Armitage had the chance to explain the exact reason for his visit.

Brane shook his head. 'There ain't no Hopecroft Road.'

'That's what the lady in the post office said. But she was certain you'd know if there was such a road fifty years ago, whose name has been changed since.'

'There's not been a Hopecroft while I've been working. Seems like someone got the name wrong, which wouldn't be anything unusual. I've had letters wrongly addressed more times than I'll ever remember and it's only on account of me using me brains that they've been delivered. People say that machines'll take on everything. What machine is going to know B. P. Smith in Mullins Street is really B. P. Smith in Murrins Street?'

'They aren't, are they?' Armitage stood. 'Thanks a lot for your help. Sorry to have bothered you.'

'Nice to have a bit of a chat . . . You're quite sure it was Hopecroft Road?'

'Seventy-Five A, Hopecroft Road.' He shook hands, crossed to the dooor.

'Hey!'

He turned.

'Seventy-Five A?'

'That's right.'

'It seems like . . .'

Armitage waited and as the minutes passed he began to think that Brane must have his senile moments as well as much brighter ones.

'Was this during the war?'

'The letter was dated nineteen-forty-two.'

'Then it's Montague Avenue you're looking for.'

'The name was changed?'

Brane shook his head and there was a sly smile on his stubbled face. 'It's still Montague Avenue.'

'I don't quite understand.'

'It was a big house, built long afore any of the others nearby. Large garden. There was this stone fountain in the centre of the lawn and in the cold weather there used to be huge icicles hanging down from it. The goldfish were the biggest I've ever seen and they used to ask for grub! I had a mate what bred maggots and I'd take some with me and when I delivered letters the fish'd see me and come up to the surface to be fed. On Sundays, the owner said they'd be real disappointed when I didn't turn up. Nice bloke, he was. Educated and all that, but no side. Suffered from asthma, same as me, which was why neither of us were in the army.'

'If the letters were addressed to Hopecroft Road, why did you deliver them to this place in Montague Avenue?'

'I couldn't say, mister. All I know is, I was told that any letter addressed to Seventy-Five A, Hopecroft Road, was to go to the big house.'

'Who told you to do that?'

'The local postmaster. Nasty little man, he was.'

'You must have been curious?'

'During the war people learned to say nowt and mind their own business. I'd me brother, Fred, and he was at sea, so I knew what careless talk could do to him; I didn't talk careless and I didn't ask questions.'

'You never had any idea of what was going on in that house?'

'Not a clue.'

'How many people lived in it?'

'There was the owner—the bloke I've told you about. And then there was a young lady and two young gentlemen who turned up every day.'

'Was there much mail?'

'Bags of it.'

'All addressed to different people?'

'As far as I can remember.'

'It all sounds a bit odd.'

'There was a lot of odd things happened during the war.'

'Did the owner have a family?'

'Not him. I did wonder if he was one of them—if you know what I mean?—but if he was, he was still a nice bloke.'

'What happened after the war?'

'He moved on; can't say where. Someone else bought the place and then it was sold again and the house was knocked down and a lot of little ones built. I've often wondered what happened to them goldfish what knew me.'

A small bungalow in the outer reaches of Bagshot seemed a strange headquarters for a naval association, but the anchor motif on the gate, the name 'Force Ten', the wind-jammer weather vane, and the flagpole, assured Armitage he had come to the right place. He was slightly surprised that Weir wore a sports jacket rather than a number one reefer.

'Come along in,' said Weir, 'there's quite a snap in the wind despite the sun.' His oval face had brown mottling which often came with considerable age, he was almost bald, and he moved awkwardly because of trouble with his right leg, but he held his back straight and his blue eyes looked sharp enough still to scan distant horizons. 'You know, it's a privilege as well as a pleasure to meet Peregrine's son.' His words were sincere, not fulsome.

They went into the sitting-room. The walls were hung with framed photographs of warships. 'Ships I served in,' said Weir. 'All of 'em long since disappeared in the breakers' yards, of course. Which is where I'm heading fast.' He chuckled as if the prospect did not really alarm him. 'Do sit down. And what'll you have to drink? There's sherry, whisky, sweet vermouth or, if you're like me, pink gin?'

Armitage chose a gin and tonic. Weir left the room, soon to return with a tray on which were two glasses and a bowl of crisps. He handed Armitage a glass, set the crisps on the glass-topped coffee table, sat. 'So what do you do in life since you didn't follow in your father's footsteps?'

'I'm a sculptor.'

It was clear that the arts had never figured largely in Weir's life. For a while conversation was general and to some degree difficult, since they had so little in common. Then Armitage introduced the reason for his visit.

'I do keep the records of the association, but I don't think they're going to be much use to you. Of course, with your father having been awarded the GM after leaving the *Waveney*, there's a special reference to him in the Commemoration Book, but I'm sure you'll know all the details . . . I've looked that out for you as I knew you'd want to see it.'

The large book was leather bound, with the ship's crest gold embossed. On the first page was a photograph of her steaming at full speed in calm waters, leaving an ever broadening wake. On the second page were details of her history. Commissioned in 1937, she had been torpedoed in early 1940, but had made port. Repaired and recommissioned, she had been on North Atlantic convoy duties until the end of 1941, when she had been sent to the Mediterranean. She had been sunk during the Sicilian landings. There were lists of crew members on each voyage, all handwritten in beautiful script, a list of actions, a copy of the official acceptance of a shared U-boat, and an In Memoriam (restricted to those who had died on active service). Pride of place in this last was given to Lieutenant Peregrine Armitage, GM. Armitage stared at the photograph of his father, one he had not seen before; as he read the words from the citation, he experienced a lump in his throat.

'She was a very happy ship and I like to think that it was in part the memory of her that helped your father show such outstanding bravery.'

'Did you know him?'

'I sailed with him for just the one trip and unfortunately can't claim that we were close friends. I was Guns and something was wrong with Y turret, and although we worked twenty-five hours a day, we couldn't find out what. The old man had one hell of a temper ... But the last thing you want is for me to ramble on about my wartime reminiscences.'

There was a hint of self-mockery in the way in which Weir spoke and this belied the initial impression Armitage had gained that he was a man obsessed by the past. 'Did you know that he left the ship to do intelligence work?'

'At the time we hadn't the slightest idea; just thought it was an ordinary posting.'

'Did that sort of thing happen often?'

'Can't remember another time.' He chuckled. 'Maybe because, as we used to say, anyone who went to sea was so stupid that even a colonel in the Guards would notice the fact.'

'What sort of intelligence work did he do?'

'I've no idea.'

'And I don't suppose you can suggest any reason why he was in Portugal three weeks before he was captured in France?'

'I haven't the faintest, I'm afraid . . . Will you have a refill?'

'Not for me, thanks, having to drive . . . I imagine you have the addresses of the surviving members of the crew who were on the ship that last voyage my father made?'

'They won't be up to date. Things have rather come to a standstill . . . Well, to be honest, there really isn't a Waveney Association left. Interest slowly drained away and in the end I simply didn't bother to send out subscription requests; you're the first person to show any interest in the Association in heavens know how long. In fact, something like three years ago, I got in touch with a chap at the Admiralty and asked if they'd like to take charge of all the records. He wasn't interested—the war was such a long time ago. I told him, not for the survivors it wasn't.'

'Time wears away even the grains of sand in the desert.'

'That's one way of putting it. Ought I to know where that comes from?'

'From a tribe in Sudan who have a saying for every conceivable situation and some that aren't conceivable . . . Would you give me what addresses you have? There's a chance I might find someone who could help me.'

'I will, certainly, but frankly you'll be wasting your time. You see, even five years ago, I was the only officer left alive and all the other survivors were ratings. They wouldn't have known anything about the officers because back in those days rank created a virtually insurmountable division.'

'I suppose it did . . . There's really no point in bothering, then.'

Weir looked at Armitage, took a deep breath, spoke in a rush. 'D'you think there's any chance you'd look after the records, and especially the Commemoration Book—after I'm dead, that is? It would be nice to know that when I'm gone everything won't just be thrown into the dustbin. And who would make a better guardian than the son of our only GM?'

Armitage did not hesitate. 'Of course I will. And maybe in a few years' time the Admiralty will learn enough sense to take an interest in their own past; or perhaps the Maritime Museum would be interested.'

'That's great. You've made me feel . . . well, like we'll all be living on a little even though we're buried . . .' He became silent, embarrassed by his own sentimentality.

Ten minutes later Armitage stood. 'I'd better be moving. Many thanks for all your help.'

'Not much of that, I'm afraid . . . Look, I've had an idea. Why not have a word with someone in Naval Intelligence to try to find out what you can? After fifty years, surely there's no need to keep things secret?'

CHAPTER 4

At each port of call, as he sardonically thought of them, there was a similar response to his request. First, blank amazement, next obvious indifference, and finally—when it was clear that he did not have the grace to recognize when he was not wanted—resentment, which took the form of sending him on run-around. Try the Ministry of Defence, try Records, try Mr Smith, try Mr Jones . . . But years of striving to make a living as a sculptor had armoured Armitage with a dislike of fools, a contempt for perceived authority, and a very thick skin. Finally, and following an act of capitulation, he gained an interview with a PRO.

The young man in Room 17—which had all the dusty anonymity of somewhere seldom used—had a polished manner, a supercilious smile, and the understated superiority of someone who had been educated in expensive schools. 'It is rather an unusual request, you know.'

'Possibly,' replied Armitage.

He flapped a languid hand in the air. 'I mean, it's rather like calling in at Scotland Yard and asking to speak to someone in MI6.'

'If I wanted to do that, I'd probably go to Russia.'

The young man thought that to be in poor taste. 'Perhaps you'll tell me precisely what it is you want?'

'Information. According to the official report, my father was killed in north-western France after working there for several months as an undercover agent. But recently I've come into possession of information which proves that three weeks before his death he was in Portugal.'

'And?'

'And I want to know why the official report is wrong.'

'I suppose you're writing a biography of your father?'

'That's right.'

'Exactly what is this information that proves the official records wrong?'

'A letter, written by my father.'

'You do realize, I suppose, that during a war it's often prudent not to set out the facts as they actually exist?'

'If by that you're suggesting he deliberately set up a smokescreen, yes, I am just capable of realizing that.'

'Then . . .'

'The letter was posted in Portugal; the contents make it clear that he wasn't in France.'

The young man stared wearily up at the ceiling. 'I'm sorry, but I really don't think there's anything we can usefully do to help you.'

'You could start by checking your records.'

'This does come under the remit of Intelligence. They have rules . . .'

'After fifty years, even Intelligence ought to be intelligent enough to see there can't be any point to further secrecy.'

'I fear you do not understand the nature of the matter, Mr . . .' He had forgotten.

'Armitage.'

'Mr Armitage. I'll be blunt. We won't be able to help you.'

'There's one last question. Is a widow's naval pension a state secret?'

'Of course not.'

'Then perhaps you could at least find out why my mother was paid a pension that was very considerably more than was normal for the widow of a naval lieutenant?'

The young man drummed on the desk with his fingers. He stood. 'Would you wait?'

Five minutes became ten; ten became fifteen. Armitage was about to storm out, even if that awarded victory to the other side, when the door opened and a man in his early forties, dressed in casual clothes, entered. 'So sorry to keep you waiting. My name's Jeremy Wiggins.' He shook hands with enthusiasm. 'And if I'm not very much mistaken, you're the famous sculptor?'

It was not a classification that Armitage was prepared to refute.

'I saw a work of yours last summer and fell in love with it. If I'd had the money, I'd have bought it. Should have bullied the bank manager, of course, and in twenty years' time I'm going to kick myself for not having done so.' He settled on the edge of the desk. 'I wonder if you'd just give me a run-down on the facts. I know you've already told Archie everything, but he does have a knack of getting things so hopelessly wrong.' He grinned broadly. 'Strictly between you and me, he's a PRO because that's the only job for which his lack of ability qualifies him.'

Armitage, his previous belligerent resentment largely

charmed away, explained for the second time the reason for his request.

'This letter was quite definitely posted in Portugal?'

'According to the stamp and the postmark.'

'It could, of course, have been written in France and then taken by courier to Portugal to be posted there to hide the place of origin. That sort of thing was done to help agents keep in touch with their families without compromising their positions. The house in Hanwell that you've mentioned would have been the Box Number—that's what they used to be called.'

'His work was in north-west France, keeping tabs on the ports; he was captured near Brest. The letter spoke of orange and almond trees and as far as I know there aren't many of those around Brest.'

Wiggins smiled. 'I can't argue with that . . . Do you have the letter with you?'

'No, I left it back in my mother's house.'

'Is there anything else in it which would help to pinpoint exactly where it was written?'

'It mentions the village of Exchaux and I've checked that—it's near Lisbon. The rest of the letter is very personal.'

'It does make me wonder if . . . Well, when couples are apart, especially if soon after marriage, they do sometimes try to recapture their happiness by evoking past events. Did your parents travel together anywhere where citrus and almond trees are common?'

'Their honeymoon was spent on a cruise in the Mediterranean.'

'Then here may be the possible answer. The letter was written in France and taken by courier to Portugal—hence the village—where it was posted. The orange and almond trees existed only in your father's imagination and were, if you like, a symbol of the happiness they had experienced on their honeymoon.'

'That wouldn't answer why my mother was given a

pension very much higher than she could have expected as the widow of a lieutenant.'

'Surely that was because your father was a hero?'

'This country normally forgets its heroes and their widows the moment the war's over.'

'Isn't that being rather cynical?'

'Realistic.'

'I really do hope not so . . . Look, I can quite understand that you want to clear up the apparent discrepancy in order to make the biography as accurate as possible. So I'll do what I can to check the facts. To help me, will you give me your mother's full name and address and any other details you think might be of assistance.' He slid off the desk, to stand. 'But I'll be battling against entrenched bureaucracy, so don't expect instant results!'

The calendar said it was the middle of April, the weather said it was early March. The wind was bitter, there had been rain and soon it would rain again, and everything was tinged with grey.

Armitage parked the Metro and brought out of it the three cardboard boxes he'd got from the local store that morning. He unlocked the back door of the cottage and went into the kitchen, then through the small hall to the stairs. On the first trip to his mother's bedroom, he took up two of the boxes; on the second, the third and last. Before starting work, he looked round the room, very conscious that this might well be the last time he saw it. A firm buyer had agreed to the asking price. The estate agents had told him he was very lucky to be selling so quickly. The observation had angered him. No man could be called lucky when he was selling his past.

He carried one box across to the chest-of-drawers and loaded into it the sheets from the bottom drawer which he needed at home. The middle drawer was already empty. The two top ones were half filled with a jumble of personal possessions—his mother had not been the tidiest of persons—and he began to pack these into the second box. He stopped when he picked up the photo album. He opened this. The first photograph was of his parents, outside the church on their wedding day. His mother's happiness had turned character into something very closely resembling beauty. His father looked precisely as she had always described him—a man who had never really outgrown the practical jokes of the gunroom. There followed several photos of guests at the reception, then many more of their honeymoon. Aboard a ship, playing deck quoits, dancing when the ship was rolling so that everyone was half off balance; the Rock, seen from the sea, and two shots of his mother, unusually looking apprehensive, in the close company of a Barbary Ape; Palma, also seen from the sea; a mule cart, the driver of which was fast asleep and leaving the mule to find its own way; a prickly pear cactus; a squat windmill; Llueso Bay, backed by mountains; a woman, toothless, plainly uneasy at having her photo taken; a man, identified as Pedro the Iceman, yet not quite certain what to do about a foreign tourist who had the gall to photograph him . . .

He remembered his mother's description of the trip around Mallorca. Because the Spanish Civil War had only just finished, the passengers on the liner had been strongly advised not to move beyond the centre of Palma and on no account to try to travel outside the city; food was very scarce, people were sullen and the authorities, determined to stamp out every trace of resistance and suspicious of everyone, were refusing to grant any travel permits. To present his father with a challenge was like offering red meat to a hungry dog. A fluent Castilian speaker, having been to school in Madrid for several years, he had taken a taxi to the military headquarters and there cajoled, flattered, and invoked the might of the British Navy in order to be granted the necessary permits. They had travelled the length of the island in an ancient Fiat, literally held together with wire, and had picnicked above Llueso Bay. His mother had described the bay as the garden of Eden before the advent of the Cox—she had had a robust, naval sense of humour. But then, on a honeymoon, even Bradford would sparkle . . .

His rambling thoughts were suddenly brought up short. In the letter, posted in Portugal and either written there or in France, hadn't his father mentioned Pedro the Iceman? Was this a coincidence? It seemed too far-fetched to be one. So was the reference pointing to a code within a code, which made a lie of everything? Or was the name in the letter—despite his certainty—slightly different?

He crossed to the desk and opened up the secret compartment. There was now only one envelope and it contained the block of four penny blacks. Any ordinary thief would have taken the stamps, not the letter.

CHAPTER 5

Mid-June in Mallorca was expected to be hot, but not so hot that a man perspired even as he lifted a glass of brandy to his lips . . .

There was the swishing sound of the bead curtain over the front door being pushed apart and then falling back into place; seconds later, Dolores entered the dining-room, also used as the family sitting-room, a heavy plastic shopping bag in each hand. 'Matilda's waiting in the car because there are two more bags to bring in.' She crossed through to the kitchen.

Jaime looked at Alvarez, then refilled his own glass before passing the bottle across. Alvarez filled his and added four ice cubes. As he drank, fresh beads of sweat formed on his forehead, neck and back. It was ridiculous, he thought, to expect a man to work in such heat . . .

There was the sound of a car horn.

Dolores appeared in the doorway of the kitchen. 'Perhaps

you are both so deaf that you did not hear me? Matilda is waiting in the car because there are two more bags to bring in. And perhaps you did not hear her blow the car's horn because she is in a hurry as she has to return home to prepare lunch for that husband of hers who, like all men, expects to be waited on hand and foot?'

'I've had one hell of a morning,' muttered Jaime.

She faced Alvarez. 'And no doubt you also have been working so hard you're totally exhausted? Then do not, either of you, disturb yourselves. I will collect the rest of the shopping from the car since, unlike you, I have not had an exhausting morning. All I have had to do is make and serve your breakfasts, prepare lunch in a kitchen so hot that the fires of hell would be cool by comparison, wash your dirty clothes after picking them up from the floor where you had left them, being in such a hurry to get to work, dust the bedrooms, make the beds, polish the dining-room table, take Isabel to her revision studies, see that Old Antonia is as comfortable as may be, drive with Matilda to the new supermarket to buy as much shopping as possible, no matter how heavy, because I have to save every possible peseta . . .' She walked past them and through to the front door, handsome head held high.

'She's becoming worse,' said Jaime gloomily. 'It was never like this when Franco was alive.'

That, thought Alvarez, was both right and wrong. Right because Dolores was undoubtedly becoming more imperious, no doubt encouraged by American programmes on the television which supported the bizarre proposition that the sexes were equal, wrong because even when Franco had been alive, she had been of an unusually assertive nature. Of course, Jaime should have been more of a man and taught her her place right from the beginning.

'You're lucky, not being married,' went on Jaime. 'If I had my time again . . .' He stopped as he heard the swish of the bead curtain.

She returned, if anything more weighed down than before.

She passed them without a word and once in the kitchen began to bang things around to show her displeasure. Juan and Isabel came in from the street and asked how much longer lunch was going to be and were immediately sent upstairs to wash and tidy themselves, much to their annoyance.

Strangely, during the course of the meal, Dolores's bad temper gradually abated and by the time they ate the sweet—bananas and almonds—she was quite relaxed. 'Enrique, can you do something for me this afternoon?' she asked, as she peeled a banana.

'Of course,' Alvarez replied, eager to promote her good humour.

'It won't take long.'

'It doesn't matter. There's nothing important going on.'

'No?' A touch of ice returned to her voice. 'But I thought that before lunch you were completely exhausted because you'd had to work so hard?'

'I . . . I managed to finish it all; that's why it was so hard?'

She ignored the weak answer. 'D'you know where Ca'n Pyloto is?'

He shook his head.

'It's up the Laraix valley, not far from the deserted village which is being restored. Cousin Francisca has just moved in and I want you to take something to her.'

Jaime looked up. 'Who's Cousin Francisca? I've never heard of her before.'

'There are an endless number of people you've never heard of.'

'But you've only got five cousins and . . .'

'She is not a true cousin, but that is what I like to call her. Do you object?'

'No, of course not.' He smiled weakly. 'Is she married?'

'Her husband died two years ago. He was a most unusual man. He died from overwork.'

Isabel giggled.

Alvarez put a couple of toasted almonds in his mouth and as he chewed them, he carefully considered what he'd just heard. Cousin or no true cousin, Francisca wouldn't be the first widow to whom Dolores had introduced him. It was a strange fact that women were forever complaining about the burdensome toils of marriage, yet were forever ready to enmesh their sisters in such toils . . .

Dolores might have read his mind. 'There's no need to do anything more than just drop the things. In fact, it'll be much the best if you come straight away. Her husband was such a good man when he was younger.'

'What's that to do with Enrique clearing out quickly?' asked Jaime in perplexed tones.

'She might find any comparison painfully odious.'

Alvarez awoke and stared up at the ceiling; then, reluctantly, he climbed off the bed and dressed. He went along to the bathroom and turned on the cold tap to rinse his face, but there was only a brief dribble of water. He swore. Every summer there was less water available to the village because more was diverted from the restricted resources down to the port so that the foreign tourists should not go short. He made his way down to the kitchen.

Dolores had set out on the table a small framed print of the Virgin Mary, a loaf of bread, a small packet of salt, a dried sardine, and a tomato. 'Don't forget to wish her Many Years as you give her these.'

It was the traditional gift to someone moving into a new home. A custom that was, sadly, falling into disuse because happiness was now more often equated with television and videos than symbolically expressed spiritual values.

She carefully packed the items into a small cardboard box which she wrapped with gift paper. 'Tell her they are from the Ramez family.'

'Won't she know who I am?'

She shrugged her shoulders. 'I may just have mentioned you to her, I may not.'

He cheered up. It seemed that she was not bent on matchmaking. 'Precisely where along the valley is her place?'

'A kilometre this side of the deserted village. The house is set back and there are some fruit trees growing in front of it. She said she's going to ask the man who works in the garden of the next house belonging to some wealthy Germans to keep the place tidy.'

'Right, then, I'll get moving.'

He left the house. His nearly new Seat Ibiza was parked almost immediately outside. He put the box on the front passenger seat, settled behind the wheel, turned the key, and as the engine fired immediately he experienced renewed pride in this possession—one to which, even a few years back, he could never have aspired.

He drove round the block, over the torrente—bone dry, as it had been since March—and out on to the Laraix road. Half way along the valley, he turned left on to a track, recently metalled. The farmland on either side was good, if not as rich as that around Mestara, and there was plenty of water, most of it no more than twenty metres down. Until recently a large proportion of the farmers had lived in the village and come out to their land each day, so that there were not many old houses; but of new houses there was a plenitude because the valley was a favourite with those foreigners who preferred not to live too cheek-by-jowl. Some years ago he'd heard of a small caseta with a hectare of land for sale and he had daydreamed of buying it—but the price had been 200,000 pesetas and that had been a king's ransom; today, that property would cost 30 million and for him it still represented a king's ransom. As the old Mallorquin saying had it, 'The poor man never catches the stage-coach, but always stays with the mule cart.'

He passed a villa, clearly owned by a foreigner since the garden grew flowers and no vegetables, and came to a field, roughly two hectares in size, that was bounded by drystone walls and in which were a great number and variety of fruit trees—orange, lemon, tangerine, grapefruit, loquat, persimmon, pomegranate, apricot, apple, plum, and fig. He braked the car to a stop in front of wrought-iron gates. A wooden board named the property Ca'n Pyloto. Dolores had off-handedly spoken of 'some fruit trees'—this was an orchard!

He left the car to open the gates, drove on to the rough dirt track which led down to the house. This was one of the few old ones in the valley, traditional in shape, originally part stables or cowshed, built from stone and to the simplest design in which there had been no place for visual appeal. Above the front patio a vine grew across a wire trellis and dozens of bunches of grapes, as yet only half size, hung down. He opened the front door, stepped inside, and called out. 'Señora.'

The entrance hall was, as was customary, also a reception room which was used only on formal occasions. It was lightly furnished, but the two chairs and round table were antique, while set in the walls were ancient, attractive tiles depicting country pursuits; the carpet—an unusual addition—was large, intricately designed, and rich with colour. Cousin Francisca had clearly not been left a poor widow.

She came through the arched doorway in the middle of the far wall. She was dressed in mauve, the local traditional colour for mourning after the first year and one which suited her; even to his eyes, her dress, to which she had risked adding a little lace, was too smart to have been made in the village. Tall for a Mallorquin, firmly shaped yet not plump, her face virtually unlined, he found it impossible to place her age within ten years. 'Señora Jimenez?'

'Yes?'

'I'm Enrique, Dolores's cousin.'

'Of course! I ought to have known!' She spoke Mallorquin with a soft accent, which placed her as having been brought up somewhere to the west of the island.

'She asked me to bring you a welcome from the Ramez family.' He held out the gift-wrapped parcel.

She took it, crossed to the table, and unwrapped it.

'May you have Many Years,' he said as she opened the box.

'How nice to find old customs observed! . . . I'm sure I'm going to be very happy for many, many years. Will you say thank you very much to Cousin Dolores?'

He accepted that as a polite dismissal, a little piqued that she had not offered him a drink—that was also an old custom. He said goodbye and returned to his car. Perhaps, he thought, Dolores had talked about him much more than she'd suggested and Cousin Francisca hadn't realized how readily she exaggerated; perhaps Señora Jimenez was too grand a lady to offer hospitality to a mere inspector in the Cuerpo General de Policía.

As he drove slowly towards the gateway he saw the estanque built against the roadside wall, and the well-head to the right of it. Judging by the size of the estanque, which could well hold 100,000 litres, the well was a very productive one. With all this land, the fruit trees, and almost unlimited water, a man could produce real crops . . .

He passed through the gateway, drew into the side of the road and left the car to return to close the gates. He stared back at the house. Foreigners would have found its unaltered box shape dourly ugly, but he saw it as attractive because it was the true past and a man who kept faith with that might have faith in the future. That she had altered nothing meant that, despite a lack of manners, she must at heart be a woman of sense and understanding.

He sighed as he settled once more behind the wheel. Envy seldom played a part in his life, but he certainly envied her these two hectares of land which could so easily be made to yield, in addition to all the fruit, heavy crops of tomatoes, peppers, aubergines, beans, artichokes, cauliflowers, cabbages, peas, strawberries, sweetcorn, potatoes, groundnuts, melons, pumpkins . . .

As a member of the civil service, he should not have worked from the guardía civil post, but years ago he had been stationed there on a purely temporary basis and it had not since occurred to anyone to move him.

He passed the cabo at the front desk, who was three parts asleep, and went up the stairs to the first floor and his office, an exertion which caused him to sweat and to suffer temporary breathlessness. He sat behind the desk, stretched out, and closed his eyes. A fly began to buzz around the room, but the annoyance was not sufficient to cause him the further exertion of swatting it . . .

The telephone rang, jerking him awake. He lifted the receiver.

'Is that you, Enrique? Aren't you looking for Pedro the Simple?'

He tried to remember.

'Well?'

Of course! Pedro Segui, also known as Pedro the Simple, had been reported missing. 'Have you found him?'

'That's right.'

'Who's that speaking?'

'Who d'you think it is, you stupid old bastard? Julio.'

'Is he dead?'

'Sweet Mary, but they don't employ you for your brains! Of course he's dead when he looks just like that calf of mine that broke its neck and I didn't find it for a month.'

'How can you be certain it's him if he's in that sort of a state?'

'Who else goes around in a skirt?' The connection was abruptly cut.

CHAPTER 6

A plain stretched from Llueso to the bay, but this was not unbroken; a few low hills rose out of it at irregular intervals and Yanez's large finca lay immediately to the south of one of these.

Alvarez drove off the road on to a dirt track, rough enough to cause him to slow almost to a walking pace in order not to stress the suspension of the car. The track wound its way past fields of stubble—without irrigation, nothing more could be grown until autumn—and through a belt of fruit trees to come to the house. This, like Ca'n Pyloto, was traditional in style, but it was completely unreformed and one end still housed cattle. Near to it was a stone-built barn; beyond the far end, an open-sided shed. Chickens were scratching about in the dirt and the arrival of the car sent them scattering. He climbed out. This was the true countryside and the nearest tourist could well have been a hundred kilometres away. He could hear pigs grunting and occasionally squealing and a humming bird hawk-moth, with wings a blur of motion, using its proboscis to sample the flowers of a lantana bush; pigeons were perched on the roofs and their constant bows made them look like a row of heavily bosomed, gossiping women; house martins, whose nests were under the eaves, were working at a frantic pace to keep their families fed; a tethered goat, standing in the shade of a fig tree, viewed the world with disdain.

The front door opened and an ibicenco hound came bounding out, to the accompaniment of a barrage of curses; it barked at Alvarez as it circled him, then turned and sniffed the rear nearside tyre of the Ibiza before lifting its leg. Yanez came out of the house. Roughly the same age as Alvarez, he was dressed in singlet and shorts, both heavily dirt-stained.

'Keep your dog off my car,' said Alvarez.

'Does it good.'

'If it strips the paint, I'll send you the bill.'

Yanez, two days' stubble darkening his chin, grinned.

'So what's that in there?' Alvarez jerked his head in the direction of a tractor in the open-sided shed.

'What's it look like?'

'Like you're another rich farmer.' He walked past the

house to the shed to examine the gleaming new tractor that looked powerful enough to work the American prairies.

Yanez came and stood by his side. 'You don't talk any less daft. These days a man has to work himself to death to keep his stomach half filled.'

'So how can you afford something that must have cost a million?'

'One?' He spoke scornfully. 'With all the equipment, five.'

'You pay five million for a tractor that's twice the size you need and you can say you aren't rich?'

'Didn't pay for most of it, did I?'

'They're giving 'em away these days, I suppose?'

'That's right.'

'And I'm a Basque from Cadiz.'

'Someone told me this Common Market thing was asking farmers what they want, so I went along to the town hall and said I wouldn't mind a new tractor.'

'There are surely more fools than wise men in the world! . . . All right, so they gave you the money. Why didn't you buy a smaller one that would have fitted your fields?'

'Because it's bigger'n Jordi's,' he said with glee. 'Look, I ain't got all day to stand around and talk. D'you want to see old Pedro, or don't you?'

'All right, all right. How d'you come to find him?'

'One of the lambs went missing, so I went up top to see if it had wandered there. There's still no sign of the bloody thing.' It was clear that the missing lamb was far more important to him than the discovery of a corpse.

'Shall we move, then?'

'What have I been bloody well trying to get you to do?' He strode off, his dog excitedly scouting ahead of them. For two hundred metres the land rose only gently, then it became steep. Hundreds of years ago the hillside had been terraced and planted with olive trees; within the past forty years such marginal farming had become uneconomic and so when part of one of the rock walls collapsed, it was no longer repaired—there were even times when the ripe olives weren't harvested because the labour of knocking them down with bamboo poles could cost more than they would fetch.

Before they were half way up, Alvarez was breathless; by the time Yanez reached the crest, he was more than a hundred metres behind.

'D'you need a hand?' Yanez shouted scornfully.

He longed to rest, but pride forced him to struggle on.

'My four-year-old grandson could race you,' said Yanez, as Alvarez finally reached his side.

Alvarez was far too exhausted to reply, and as he wiped the sweat from his face and waited for his heartbeats to slow to a safer rhythm, he promised himself that he really would give up smoking and cut right back on his drinking; perhaps even attend the newly-opened gymnasium in the village and exercise himself back into condition.

The top of the hill, about a hectare in size, was almost level and it had been planted with olive trees; these, enjoying a deeper soil than those on the terraces, were larger and less convoluted in shape. Beyond them, and in sharp contrast to the southern approach, was a rock face and on the ground below there were boulders of many sizes which had fallen in the past.

Alvarez, who had not realized the nature of the land on the far side, stepped up to the edge and looked down. Unfortunately, he was faced by a sheer five-metre drop. He suffered an immediate attack of vertigo and for a second, which seemed like a minute, he felt as if he were being propelled forward into a fall. Somehow he broke through his terror and stepped back.

'Now what's up?' demanded Yanez.

'I . . . I suffer from altophobia.'

'If you ask me, there ain't much you don't suffer from.'

He had learned over the years how to bring his fear under control provided the depths which faced him were not too great. Slowly, very carefully, breathing deeply as he assured himself that he couldn't possibly slip, he stepped forward until he could once more look down.

There was a natural rock shelf, perhaps two metres wide and eight metres long, and roughly in the centre of this lay a body, one arm outstretched, the other bent under himself. He wore a kilt and it was this that made it virtually certain the dead man was Pedro Segui.

For as long as memory reached, he'd been known to everyone as Pedro the Simple. In the days when naked power had ruled the land and men had disappeared for no better reason than that they had suggested that perhaps it was wrong that a few should have so much while the majority had so little, he had shown himself to be a fool. He had behaved as if there was no cause to fear; when others had spoken only after thinking thrice, he had spoken without thought; when to query was to criticize and to criticize was to engage suspicion, he had queried everything. It was his stupidity which saved him; a fool licensed to be foolish. He had become a mascot to the soldiers, to be given food and even occasionally the few odd céntimos to buy a beer, since there was the time when he could no longer make a living by selling ice because his mule had been commandeered and the ice-making machine had broken down and spare parts were unobtainable. He amused the soldiers and they were grateful to anyone who did that.

When the first tourists had begun to arrive, they had demanded ice. Since domestic refrigerators had not yet become available, the village ice-making machine had been repaired with parts expensively smuggled in from France and he had carried the ice around on a hand cart. Soon, he'd made enough money to buy a mule; then to employ a thirteen-year-old youth and to buy a second mule. He'd made more money than he'd known existed and he gave most of it away because it made people so happy to receive it. Which generosity, of course, confirmed his stupidity.

Domestic refrigerators appeared in the shops and cabinets

containing bags of ice at the newly built petrol stations. Trade slumped and it became clear even to him that one mule would have to be sold, but he put off the day for as long as possible because when it went the youth too would have to go. The latter, no longer so young, resolved the problem by announcing one morning that he wasn't going to work another minute for a dippy old fool, earning only céntimos, when he'd found himself a job in a new tourist hotel from which he could expect many pesetas.

Trade had continued to slump until only a few old and faithful customers had bought from him. Finally, it had ceased altogether because the village ice-making plant closed down. He hadn't seemed to mind. He had no money—no one ever explained the slowly developing welfare state to him—but he laughed a lot and seemed content and people gave him food and pesetas because they needed to believe that there was still laughter and contentment in the world just as much as had the conscript soldiers many years before. And one day a Scotsman from Aberdeen, at the conclusion of thirteen days' drinking, had given him a kilt in the MacGregor tartan. He'd worn this all the time because he loved the colours and it made people laugh . . .

Alvarez came to a stop. He'd had no idea that anyone still lived in such squalid circumstances and he knew a quick anger that this should be. Then it occurred to him that perhaps Pedro had been so simple that he had not understood he was living in squalor because the sight of other men's riches had not bred in him the canker of jealousy.

The walls of the small, low building were built of rock, held together only with Mallorquin cement so that in a few places they had begun to fall away; the two windows were unglazed; the outside door was made from plywood that had warped and the roof from broken panels of corrugated plastic recovered from some rubbish tip; the floor was earth; in the first room, the bed was an alcove with a stone base on which had been laid a tatty mattress filled with straw and there was one rickety table and one rickety chair, rough wooden shelves on which was a collection of tins, mostly rusty, and a small television. Since the place was not connected to electricity and the set was not battery operated, it could not have worked. Presumably, Pedro had stared at the screen and mentally filled it with images of a world in which there was only happiness.

Alvarez walked back up the dirt track, past a maquis of grass, brambles, cistus, rosemary, rose-bay willow-herb and pine trees, to the road where he'd parked his car and he drove to the nearest house, five hundred metres along the road.

The woman who opened the front door looked flustered and careworn; her obvious pregnancy and the appearance of twins and a slightly older sister suggested that she had every cause to do so. He identified himself and apologized for troubling her.

'That's all right,' she answered, in heavily accented Spanish. One of the twins began to thump the other and there were screams. 'Pack it in or I'll murder both of you,' she said in English as she grabbed the thumper. 'I'm sorry about the noise,' she said in Spanish.

'There's no need to worry,' he replied in English.

'Oh my God, you understood! And you're a detective!'

He smiled. 'Señora, I rather doubt you really intend to murder your children.'

She hesitated, then smiled back at him. 'There are times when it would be all too easy . . . Come on in, but mind you don't trip over anything.'

It was a bungalow, on ground sufficiently high for there to be a view to the bay. The sitting-room, with open-plan dining-room to one side, faced south; the picture windows were protected from the sun by a roofed patio. The room was littered with playthings and she began hurriedly to clear some rag books off the settee, but stopped when her daughter sidled up to her and whispered. She said, 'No,' in an embarrassed voice, reached out to pick up the last two books. 'Would you like to sit there?'

He sat. The daughter stared at him thumb in mouth. 'What's your name?' he asked.

She uncorked her thumb. 'Eulalia.'

He switched to Spanish. 'It's a very pretty name.'

She giggled.

'I wouldn't have chosen it,' said her mother, 'but it's the family name and Claudio said we must use it. I think it's daft, giving the same name to every generation. You never know who's being talked about . . . Sorry, I shouldn't criticize. Claudio says I'm always criticizing. But sometimes . . .' She became silent.

It did not need much perspicacity on Alvarez's part to realize that this was yet one more marriage between a Mallorquin man and a British woman which suffered more than its fair share of misunderstandings. Experience proved that it was not a happy combination. 'Señora, you are very busy so I will be as brief as possible. I believe it was you who reported Pedro Segui to be missing?'

'That's right. Have you found him? Is he all right?'

'Sadly, he is dead.'

Her daughter came up and she ruffled her hair. 'I was afraid it might be like that.'

'Will you tell me why you reported him as missing?'

'Why I did?' The question seemed to puzzle her. 'Well, it was just . . . The thing is, I always felt so sorry for him and used to try and help. Claudio didn't like that and said I shouldn't go near him because he wasn't safe with kids. But he was just a kid himself and would never have done them any harm . . . Well, he hadn't been along for a day or two and so I went up to his place to see if he was all right and he wasn't around. I gave it another day and still there was no sign of him and that got me worried. I asked around at one or two places which used to give him some grub and they hadn't seen him, so I told the municipal police.'

'Had you any reason to think that maybe someone could have hurt him?'

'Nothing like that . . . Here, are you saying his death wasn't natural?'

'I'm afraid that at the moment that's a possibility, even though at first sight it appears to have been an accidental fall. Nothing can be certain until the post-mortem's carried out, but I examined his body and caught up in his thumbnail were some hairs which looked a different colour from the few he had left on his own head.'

'You're saying someone else was there when he died?'

'If they prove not to have been his hairs, it would seem somebody probably was. Perhaps he began to fall and grabbed for support and all he managed to get hold of was the other person's hair.'

'But that doesn't mean it wasn't an accident, does it?'

'Why did this other person not call for help?'

She instinctively drew her daughter closer to herself.

'It happened on private land and, like all farmers, Julio does not welcome strangers because he fears they may be stealing from him. Many years ago he found Pedro on one of his fields. Pedro said he was looking at butterflies, Julio did not believe him and threatened to shoot him if ever he found him on his land again. Would you think that such a threat would have scared Pedro very much?'

'I'm sure it would.'

'Then probably he would not normally have gone near the land.'

'But who on earth could possibly want to kill him?'

'That is something I shall have to discover if it becomes certain that the hairs were not his. Will you tell me now what you know about him?'

'Not very much, really. He used to talk a lot, but it was so confused it was often difficult to understand. I mean, he could start a sentence on one subject and finish it on another. I can't say I always bothered to make sense of it.'

'Did he ever mention anyone who might have held a grudge against him?'

'No. But haven't you just said that the farmer threatened him?'

'Julio always talks much louder than he acts . . . Did Pedro have many visitors?'

'Most people didn't want to have anything to do with him. They're so superstitious and they think that bad luck's catching; and anyway, these days they've become so contemptuous of anyone who's poor. They used to be cruel to him, laughing and mocking what he said and did. When Claudio discovered I'd been giving him food . . .' She stopped, unwilling to be disloyal to her husband.

One of the twins suddenly began to cry and after only the briefest of pauses, the other followed suit.

He stood. 'Señora, I have taken up too much of your time.'

She went over to the twins and tried to hush them. 'You wouldn't like to take these two with you, would you?'

'I regret that I would not know what to do with them. I am a bachelor.'

'All the gain and none of the pain, as an old boyfriend of mine used to say.'

He thanked her and left. He was seated in the Ibiza and about to start the engine when he saw her hurry out of the bungalow, obviously to say something more to him. He climbed out.

Trailing children like the Pied Piper, she came up. 'I've just remembered. Some time ago, like maybe five or six weeks, a car drove up and the driver, an Englishman, asked if I knew where Pedro the Iceman lived. I said I didn't. Then I remembered that Pedro used to sell ice and I asked him if he meant Pedro the Simple.'

'And did he?'

'It seemed like maybe he did.'

'He knew Pedro?'

'Not from the sound of things. He said something about

wanting to talk to him because of an old photo, but the twins were being extra difficult and I couldn't pay much attention.'

'Does he live on the island?'

'I wouldn't think so from the way he talked. And he was driving a tourist car.'

'Can you describe him?'

'Well . . . He was a big man—mostly bone, but maybe just a little middle-aged spread. And he had a beard which, if he'd been anything to do with me, I'd have taken a pair of shears to. I like beards, but only if they're neat.'

'How was he dressed?'

'Very casually. Like everyone else. But there's one more thing about him I do remember. He'd very blue eyes. The kind of eyes to make a woman . . .' She giggled. 'I'll tell you one thing. If I had an older daughter, I'd keep an eye on her if he was anywhere around.'

Alvarez gained the impression that if she were on her own, she might not be so careful. 'Can you remember what kind of hair he had?'

'Ordinary brown with a touch of grey; like the beard, it needed cutting.'

'You have a very good memory, señora . . . Did he visit Pedro?'

'I can't say. I mean, I had to leave home soon after I'd spoken to him to go shopping and I didn't see him again.'

'You didn't ask Pedro whether he'd met this Englishman?'

'As a matter of fact, I did, yes. But all Pedro would talk about was when he'd sold ice at fifty céntimos a half-block.'

'That must have been a long time ago.'

'A hell of a long time, judging by what it cost to buy ice last summer when our fridge broke down.'

He thanked her again for her help, said goodbye to the children—the twins ignored him, the girl hid behind her mother's skirts—and drove off.

CHAPTER 7

The forensic laboratory in Palma rang at 11.15 on Wednesday morning. 'About the hairs you sent us . . . We've checked all the usual things—roots, colour, average diameter of the medulla, and the medullary index—and can say that very probably the incident hairs came from a different head than the comparison hairs.'

'You can't be positive?'

'Not without submitting them to the latest DNA tests and that means Madrid. And before we can send them there, we need a special authority from you so that you bear the cost, not us.'

'I don't know how the superior chief would react to that.'

'Then until you do, it'll have to remain "very probably".'

After the call was over, Alvarez drummed on the desk with his fingers. Then he dialled Palma and asked to speak to Superior Chief Salas. There was a long wait before Salas, typically eschewing any greeting, snapped: 'Well?'

'Señor, I have just heard from the laboratory regarding the Segui case. The comparison of hairs—'

'What case?'

'Concerning the death of Pedro Segui.'

'I know nothing about that.'

Belatedly, Alvarez realized that he had forgotten to send a preliminary report to Palma. 'You haven't, señor? But I put my report in the post on Monday and you should have received it yesterday.'

'One moment.' There was a long pause. 'There's nothing arrived here.'

'The post really is getting even worse. The other day I'd been expecting a letter from a cousin and it hadn't arrived, so I rang—'

'I hardly think we need concern ourselves with your private affairs.'

'Of course not, señor,' he replied, satisfied that he'd managed to divert the superior chief's mind away from the missing report.

'What are the details of the case?'

He gave a brief résumé of the facts, finished by saying: 'So we need to be quite certain whether or not the hairs came from his own head or someone else's.'

'Is there any certainty they became caught up in his nail immediately prior to his death?'

'No, señor.'

'Then this might well have happened some time previously. From the sound of him, he was not the kind of man to have bothered about personal cleanliness; a distressing trait of so many islanders.'

'I wouldn't say that . . .'

'The dead man was an idiot?'

'That rather depends on how you define "idiot".'

'I should prefer not to rely on you for a definition. You make a point of the fact that the dead man would not willingly have gone on the land because of an incident which happened in the past. Your mistake is to assume that his mind would have worked so logically. A man with disturbed mental faculties thinks in a disturbed fashion . . . A murder such as this would require a motive. Have you uncovered one?'

'No, señor. But there is that rather strange incident of the Englishman who asked about him.'

'The evidence, as you've presented it, suggests he was a tourist. In which case, he will have returned to Britain many weeks ago.'

'Why should a tourist even know of Pedro's existence?'

'There is probably a very simple explanation. It is very much to be regretted that even now, after all I have said in the past, you seem determined to seek mystery where there patently is none.'

'There is something else, señor.'

'What?'

'When the señora asked Pedro about the Englishman, Pedro started talking about the time when ice had cost fifty céntimos a half-block.'

'You can find the slightest significance in that?'

'Isn't it probable that his answer to the señora was directly connected with the Englishman?'

'I have to confess to experiencing very great difficulty in imagining what possible connection even you can believe there to be between a visiting British tourist and a distant time when a block of ice cost a peseta.'

'No, señor, when half a block cost fifty . . . Oh, I see.'

'Do you? It would make my burden much lighter if only you could learn to differentiate between those facts which are, or may become, relevant and those which quite clearly are and always will be totally irrelevant. The Galicians have a saying which I recommend to you. A far-sighted farmer ploughs a straight furrow. Do you understand the meaning?'

'What happens if there are trees in the middle of the field?'

'In Galicia they do not have trees in the middle of fields. Make certain that there is a copy of your report on my desk tomorrow morning.'

'Yes, señor . . . I think the hairs caught up in the dead man's nail should be tested by the new DNA system so that we can be certain whether or not they came from his head. While I accept that they could date back to a time prior to his death, the law of probabilities suggests—'

'The law of probabilities is not one about which I am prepared to accept your construction. The tests in question are extremely expensive and therefore to be used only in cases of importance. When a man, known to be an idiot, dies and there is not even the suspicion of a motive for his murder, then it is highly probable that his death was the accident it appears to have been.'

'You don't want me to pursue the investigation any further?'

'I want your report on my desk tomorrow morning.'

'It will be there, señor. Always providing that the post office does not lose it again.'

The sopas Mallorquinas was rich, tasty, and almost a meal on its own; the bacalao a la cazuela would have astonished anyone who believed that salted cod was a food fit only for hungry cats; the flan bore no relation to its commercially made namesake. By the time the meal was finished, both Jaime and Alvarez were slightly glassy-eyed from over-indulgence.

Jaime topped up his glass, pushed the bottle of brandy across the table to Alvarez. Dolores, who'd noticed too late what he was doing, said crossly to Isabel: 'What are you waiting for? Start clearing the table.'

'But it's not my turn, it's Juan's.'

'Kindly do as I say.'

Juan spoke jeeringly and Isabel, momentarily too angry to guard her tongue, called him a name that should not have been in her vocabulary.

'What did you say?' demanded Dolores wrathfully.

Jaime chuckled.

She swung round. 'How very typical!' She placed her hands on her hips. 'My husband finds it amusing that his daughter talks like an Andaluz gipsy!'

'Steady on. It doesn't mean anything.'

'It means that she's learned a disgusting word from you two.'

'Here, why blame us?'

'Because after the third coñac you lose all control over your tongues.' She half-turned. 'Isabel, although the word you used is one that, unfortunately, you hear all too often in this house because neither your father nor your uncle has learned to guard his tongue after many brandies, if I ever hear you speak it again, I'll wash your mouth out with kitchen soap. Do you understand?'

'Yes, Mama.'

'Then now you will help me clear the table.' She went forward and began to stack the plates. 'Jaime.'

'Yes?' he answered hurriedly.

'Later on, I want you to drive me to Cousin Francisca's.'

'D'you mean this afternoon?'

'Are your wits so befuddled by coñac that you imagine I'm talking about yesterday afternoon?'

'But I told you earlier, I have to go to Palma.'

'How typical! You expect to be waited on hand and foot, yet let me make but one small request and you find a dozen reasons for not doing it.'

'That's not fair.'

She ignored him and carried the pile of plates towards the kitchen. Jaime reached for the bottle. 'You've had more than enough already,' she snapped.

Alvarez, eager to sweeten Dolores's temper, said: 'Look, if Jaime can't take you, why don't I?'

'I suppose you could,' she replied doubtfully. 'I've made empanadas for supper and cooked some extra because I know she likes them; with all the bother of settling in, she can't have much time for cooking.'

'Then I'll take you after a siesta.'

'Why not?' said Jaime. 'There's nothing like being pleasant to a woman with property; gets your feet under her table quicker.'

She was furious. 'Must you be so swinishly stupid?'

'You keep telling Enrique he ought to get married.'

'Cousin Francisca is hardly likely to consider a man who teaches his niece gutter language.'

They passed the three watermills at different levels on the side of a hill which, before they had been reformed and turned into houses, had been worked by the water from a strong spring which, illogically, surfaced just below the crest. 'I've always wanted to live in this valley,' Dolores said.

'I never knew that.' Alvarez was grateful that Dolores's ill temper seemed finally to have evaporated.

'If Jaime liked living in the countryside and we had the money . . . Farmers would be wealthy if sheep fed themselves.'

'That's true enough.'

'When I was a youngster I had a great-uncle who owned a finca at the far end, close to the mule track which goes over the mountains to Estart. I used to play in the big barn and it was all wonderfully exciting . . . It's a beautiful valley and Cousin Francisca is a fortunate woman.'

'Since she owns the house, sure. But don't forget that she's only here because her husband's dead.'

'But, the good Lord forgive me for saying this, perhaps his death was not so tragic for her as it would have been if he . . .' She stopped.

'You said he was a good man.'

'So he was, once. Maybe all men are good, once upon a time. But I doubt that.'

They turned the corner and this brought them into view of the remaining length of the valley and the mountains which enclosed its northern end. 'What was his trouble, then?' he asked.

'She's not the kind of woman to complain, but from one or two things she's said . . . There were times when he'd be away and on his return wouldn't say where he'd been.'

'Warming his fingers in another honeypot?'

'Enrique,' she said reproachfully rather than angrily, 'could you try not to be so crude?'

They left the road and drove along the track to the finca. After he'd opened the gates, they continued on down to the house.

'There's no need for you to come in,' she said, as she reached over to the back for the basket in which were the empanadas. 'I won't be long.'

Through the windscreen he watched her cross to the front door and try to open it, only to find it locked. She went round the house and out of sight. He turned and studied the land, seeing it not as it was, but as it could be if cultivated by a man who was happy to work hard. The thirstiest crops near the estanque, so that as little water as possible was lost along the irrigation channels. Or, if this were feasible, an automatic irrigation system which would allow each crop to be planted in a position which best suited it . . .

She returned, without the basket. 'Cousin Francisca is out, so I've left the basket where she can see it, but it's in the shade. Later on, I'll telephone to make certain she finds it.'

He backed and turned, drove up towards the gates, but stopped when fifty metres short of them.

'What's the matter?' she asked.

'I was just wondering how much water the estanque holds.'

As he walked into the post, the duty cabo said: 'Palma's been shouting for you. You're to ring the superior chief's office.'

'What's the trouble?'

'How would I know? Like as not, they're wondering where you've been for the past month.'

He went up to his office, sat behind the desk, and stared at the telephone. Life must have been very much easier for an inspector before the telephone had been invented . . . He lifted the receiver and dialled.

'I have a message for you from the superior chief,' the secretary said in the satisfied tones of an underling giving orders in the name of a superior. 'An incident has been reported in Maranitx and you are to go there and—'

He interrupted her. 'Señorita, Maranitx is not in my area.'

'The superior chief is naturally well aware of that. The matter concerns a foreigner and therefore he thinks you should handle it. Señor Gaspari reported a burglary—'

He interrupted her a second time. 'What nationality is this señor?'

'I understand that he is an Italian.'

'Regretfully, I do not speak Italian. So there can be no point in—'

'The local inspector reports that the señor is behaving very strangely. Early this morning he reported that his house had been broken into and his life was in great danger, yet when the inspector arrived to conduct an investigation, he said that there was no need to bother any further in the matter.'

'Then why do so?'

She spoke impatiently. 'The superior chief naturally wishes to understand why the señor has changed his story.'

'Why doesn't he tell the local inspector to question the señor and find out?'

'The inspector has only recently been transferred from the Peninsula and he has had no experience of foreigners. He finds it impossible to understand them.'

'One can deal with them for thirty years and still not do so.'

'You are to go there immediately.'

'I'm working flat out as it is—'

'The name of the house is Sa Serra.'

As he replaced the receiver, Alvarez sighed. Maranitx was in the mountains and a good fifty kilometres away— the drive would take over an hour. Unfortunately, though, it was not yet late enough for him to put off the visit until the following morning on the grounds that he could not make the double journey in the time reasonably available. This meant that he was going to be late home for supper. The family might well over-indulge themselves on the empanadas and not leave him his fair share.

CHAPTER 8

Maranitx was a small, straggling village, situated on the north side of the mountains and distantly overlooking the sea; in the summer, its setting was dramatically picturesque and many a tourist dreamed of owning a property amid such wild beauty, but in the winter, with a northerly gale bringing in banks of sullen clouds and stinging rain, the scene became harsh and even threatening.

Sa Serra was the only house in a small valley, some four kilometres from the village. Not big enough to be called manorial, yet it was larger than the average farmhouse, mainly because the adjoining barn—now incorporated—had been unusually big. Seventy-five years ago, it would have been occupied by a farmer who worked from dawn to dusk to wrest a living from the stony ground, enclosed by the mountains into a small world from which he might not venture in his mule cart more than a couple of dozen times in a year. Even now, when a car made travel to the outside world simple and quick, the Italian who lived there surely had to be a man who was less than gregarious.

The dirt track, as straight as an arrow, led up to the house between fields which were littered with stones of all sizes despite the generations of men and women who had toiled for endless hours to clear them, constructing the many walls as they did so. There was no garden, such as was usually found at a foreigner's home—only a few rose-bushes, hard pressed to survive, and several plumbago bushes in full flower. As Alvarez climbed out of the car he was able to see, behind and beyond the corner of the house, part of a swimming pool. He crossed to the front door and knocked. A middle-aged woman with a lined face set in a sour, disgruntled expression opened the door. He asked if Señor

Gaspari was in, identified himself. 'The señor reported a break-in and said his life was endangered.'

'He's told the other inspector that it was all a mistake.'

'D'you mean there was no attempt to break-in?'

'It adds up to no more than a broken shutter and window.'

'He obviously fears there may be more trouble.'

'I've told you, it's all over.'

'Nevertheless, I'd like a word with him.'

She stared angrily at him for a moment and he expected her to continue to argue, then she shrugged her broad shoulders. 'Suit yourself. He's by the pool.'

'Which is the best way to get to that?'

'Round the house.' She shut the door in his face.

He walked back along the drive until he could go down the side of the house. To his left, an old barn had been converted into a garage and in this was a new, large Citroën; immediately outside was a slightly scarred Peugeot 309.

The pool, half of which was now in the shadow of a mountain, was very large and it had a diving-board with two heights; beyond it and at the far side was a complex which contained changing-rooms and a barbecue area. There was a wide, tiled area surrounding the pool and this was in turn surrounded, except on the side with the complex, by a lawn of gama-grass. Two men sat on deckchairs on the grass, one in the shade of a multi-coloured sun umbrella secured through the centre of a metal table, the other in the full sun.

Alvarez came to a stop. 'Señor Gaspari?'

'Yes?' answered the man who sat in the shade. He was white-haired; his heavily featured, lugubrious face was only lightly tanned; he wore a shirt and shorts that could have been cleaner.

'My name is Inspector Alvarez of the Cuerpo General de Policía.'

'So?'

'I would like to ask you one or two questions, if that is convenient.'

'And if it isn't?'

'My dear Gio,' said the second man, in a Spanish that was more fluent and less accented than Gaspari's, 'when a policeman says "if that's convenient", a wise man hurries to change his convenience to suit.' About the same age as Gaspari, he wore only the briefest of costumes and despite his evident age, his body was taut and well muscled and there was not even the hint of an old man's belly. Obviously a sun-lover, his skin was the colour of mahogany. He turned his head. 'I think, Inspector, that an introduction on my part might be in order.' His tone mocked the formality of his words. 'Fermo Scalfaro. Like my friend, Italian by birth, Mallorquin by choice.'

Alvarez smiled briefly, immediately warming to this friendly manner that was in such sharp contrast to Gaspari's.

Gaspari said: 'What d'you want? I told the other policeman it was nothing.'

'So I understand, señor, but when you first reported the incident, did you not say that your life was in danger?'

He didn't answer.

'I believe the intruder didn't succeed in actually breaking into the house?'

'He broke the shutter and glass, but didn't open the window.'

'The window was closed?' said Alvarez, astonished that at this time of the year anyone should have a window shut. Then he remembered that he was speaking to a foreigner. 'But of course, you have air-conditioning.'

'No. The windows on the ground floor are wired to alarms.'

Twenty years ago, that would have been extraordinary, now it was merely unusual; the number of burglaries, almost all committed by thieves who needed money to finance their drug addiction, had led to some of the wealthier residents fitting their homes with alarms, but the frequency of such burglaries had not yet become so great that the majority had done so. That Gaspari had wired this house to an alarm system suggested that either he possessed a number of valuable things and/or he was unusually afraid of being burgled. 'Señor, would you tell me exactly what happened?'

'Inspector, I'm sure you'd be more comfortable sitting down,' said Scalfaro. 'I'll get you a chair.' He walked over to the pool complex, returned with a patio chair. 'Are you a sun or a shade man?'

'Shade, señor.'

He set the chair so that it was within the shade of the sun umbrella. Alvarez sat and again asked Gaspari to detail events.

Very little had really happened. Gaspari, who lived on his own—his wife had died a few years previously—had been awakened by the alarm. He had tried to use the bedside telephone to call the police, but that had proved to be dead. He had armed himself with his revolver and waited. The house had remained in complete silence. Later, he had gone downstairs. The shutters of one of the dining-room windows had been forced open and the glass in the window had been broken; after having coated the glass with glue and then stuck material on this, the intruder had struck the glass, which had shattered but, thanks to the backing, with very little noise. The alarm had sounded when the intruder had reached inside and unlatched the locking arm which activated the long bolt which secured the window. Gaspari had done what he could to secure the broken window and shutters, before returning upstairs. As soon as it had been daylight he'd checked the telephone wires and had found they had been cut where they entered the house; he had managed to reconnect them and had reported the attempted break-in.

'Señor, do you have a number of valuable things in the house?'

'No,' Gaspari answered curtly.

'Perhaps you keep a considerable amount of cash in hand?'

'No.'

'Then I wonder why he came here?'

'That's obvious. He expected to find both.'

'Yes, of course. But what puzzles me is that he seems to have known the window would be shut, since he brought with him the means to break it quietly, and such knowledge usually can only be obtained by a reconnaissance—which suggests a criminal with experience. But such a criminal would surely have checked for the presence of alarms. There would seem to be a small contradiction.'

'You're calling me a liar?'

'Of course not, señor.'

Scalfaro chuckled. 'Gio, you really must learn to be either a man of less honour, or to leap to its protection less energetically. All the Inspector is saying is that here is a point of contradictory interest. A policeman's life must be full of such interesting points . . . Isn't that so, Inspector?'

'Indeed.' Alvarez paused for a moment, then said: 'Señor Gaspari, why, when the break-in was clearly unsuccessful, did you say your life was in danger?'

'Because I was upset.'

'There was not the time, between the break-in and daylight, to consider the matter and realize that it was unlikely that your life was in danger?'

'Don't you try to get smart or it'll be the worse for you—'

Scalfaro broke into the angry words. 'Please understand and be sympathetic, Inspector. My friend is not a young man any more and so when this sort of thing happens it comes as a severe shock and it takes time to see things clearly once more. Also, and one does not need to be old to suffer this, there is always a reluctance to admit that one has been—how should this be put?—a little dramatic in one's reactions.'

'But of course, señor . . . Happily, it would seem as if there is no cause for further concern.'

'None at all. Clearly, the intruder had such a fright when

the alarm went off that he may still be running. Certainly, he will never return.'

Alvarez stood.

Gaspari finally made an effort to be polite. 'I . . . I'm sorry if I've been a bit . . . well, rude. But it has been a shock.'

'Of course, señor, and I understand completely. I'm very glad that everything now is in order . . . Oh, there is one more thing. Just in case you do not have a licence for your revolver . . .'

'Of course I have one,' snapped Gaspari, reverting to his previous manner.

'Then I do not need to suggest what preventive steps to take!' He said goodbye.

As he drove away from the house, he wondered if things were as straightforward as they now seemed. Gaspari had made a fool of himself, which presumably explained his sullenness. But when he had said, 'Don't you try to get smart or it'll be the worse for you', his tone had been vicious—as if he could be certain that that was not an empty threat. It was unusual for an ordinary citizen to be granted a licence to possess a revolver; much more unusual for a foreigner to be given such permission. And why had the intruder seemingly known he would have to break through glass if he was just the casual thief that other evidence suggested he must be?

Alvarez shrugged his shoulders. If Gaspari was content to call the matter closed, why should he be such a fool as to continue to worry about it?

CHAPTER 9

The telephone rang as the advertising break came to an end and the programme recommenced. No one moved. Dolores said: 'Isn't anyone going to answer it?'

'It won't be for me,' said Jaime.

'I'll go,' said Alvarez, without any further prompting. He found the latest soap opera from America to be badly flawed—in his experience, the rich were only genuinely friendly to those who were richer. He stood and threaded his way past the others to go into the front room.

'It's Francisca. How are you, Enrique?'

'Fine, thanks.' He pictured the land which could be made to yield so munificently. 'And how are things going with you?'

'I'm beginning to be able to settle down, thank goodness. Is Cousin Dolores in?'

'Yes, she is. I'll go and get her.'

'She's not busy?'

'Only watching the television.'

'Then there's no need to disturb her. Will you just tell her I phoned to thank her and to say how delicious the empanadas were. She really is a wonderful cook. She makes me feel nervous about asking you all along for a meal.'

'I'll bet you've really no cause to worry.'

She chuckled. 'There's a gallant bet! And she warned me not to be upset by some of the things you might say . . . If I do manage to pluck up my courage, perhaps I'll try lechona. My mother gave me a recipe that's supposed to have been brought to the island by Jaime the First. Do you think it really could have been?'

'It's the kind of possibility I never doubt because I want to believe it.'

'Spoken like a true romantic. You are a man of surprises . . . Anyway, whoever first introduced the recipe, it tastes delicious.'

Lechona happened to be one of his favourite dishes.

'I suppose I'll just have to pluck up my courage. You wouldn't be too rude if it wasn't perfect, would you?'

'Of course not.'

'Good . . . Well, a busy man like you won't want to listen

to me chatting away. Don't forget to thank Cousin Dolores for me. Goodbye.'

He returned to the other room. Dolores, without looking up, said: 'Who was it?'

'Cousin Francisca.'

She looked up. 'Did she want something?'

'Only to say how much she enjoyed the empanadas and what a wonderful cook you are.'

Dolores, who did not suffer from false modesty, was gratified, if not surprised, by the praise.

'She's hoping to ask us all to a meal when she's got everything straight in the house. It seems her mother gave her a recipe for lechona that's great. I didn't tell her it couldn't possibly be better than yours.'

'Certainly not better—but perhaps nearly as good.'

'Shall I turn the television off,' demanded Jaime, 'so you can chat more easily?'

For once, Dolores dutifully became silent.

Alvarez settled back in the chair. On the screen, one of the heroines, eyes moist with emotion, was clipping around her wrist the bracelet she'd just been given. In a make-believe world happiness was epitomized by diamonds. In the real world happiness lay in ploughing, cultivating, planting, growing, harvesting . . .

He was about to leave the office for a late mid-morning snack when the telephone rang. 'This is Comisario Orifla speaking.'

He had never met Orifla, but knew of him by reputation. A typical Barcelonian who was forever making a damned nuisance of himself because he'd never learned to let sleeping dogs lie.

'This morning I was instructed by the Superior Chief to conduct investigations into an incident at Sa Serra in Meranitx. You were there yesterday evening, weren't you?'

'Yes, señor. I talked to Señor Gaspari—'

'I have seen the señor this morning. Clearly, this is a

straightforward attempted break-in that failed. Therefore the case can be concluded. You agree?'

'On the face of things, yes.' A spirit of perversity—considering his conclusion of the previous evening—gripped him. 'The only thing is . . . Well, it's nothing definite, but there are one or two inconsistencies. If the thief was a casual, why did he carry and use professional gear to smash the window? If he was a pro, why hadn't he discovered the target wasn't a rich one and how did he miss the alarm system? Why was the señor's immediate reaction to fear for his life when there was no apparent cause to think the intruder would attack him?'

'All questions which can be answered simply.'

'Yet when something doesn't quite add up . . .'

'One needs to blame one's addition, not the figures. This was a simple attempted burglary that failed.'

'As you say, señor. But I do wonder why Señor Gaspari has a permit for a revolver?'

'The question does not lie within your province. The case is closed.' Orifla added a curt goodbye, rang off.

Alvarez scratched his neck where a mosquito bite was irritating. It was odd that having ordered him the previous evening to drive over to question Gaspari, Salas should then detail Orifla to take charge of the case, even before any report had been made. Even odder that a comisario should have been called in to take over a case that appeared on the evidence to be of no consequence.

He left the office, went downstairs into the street and up to the old square. The tourists were sitting and drinking at the tables set out by the three cafés which fronted the square. Recently, a far-left candidate had referred to all tourists as parasites who sucked the life blood of the islanders. Intemperate language for a local election, yet surprisingly effective because it had been seen to contain a kernel of truth within its shell of rhetoric. The tourists were able to lead their life of conspicuous leisure only at the expense of the native population.

The barman in the Club Llueso did not bother to ask him what he wanted, but filled a container with ground coffee and clipped this into the espresso machine, then poured out a very generous brandy. One never knew when it might be advisable to be on friendly terms with a policeman.

Alvarez sat by one of the windows. He drank some of the coffee and then topped it up with brandy. He lit a cigarette and thought about what had happened and became slightly bewildered by his reactions to those events. Last night, he had been more than content to accept that the case be closed. This morning, Comisario Orifla had said that it definitely was closed. But instead of gratefully forgetting the whole affair, here he was, puzzling over minor inconsistencies . . . He returned to the bar for a second brandy.

He telephoned Palma and asked to speak to an assistant in the government department which dealt with gun licences. He identified himself and said: 'Look, will you do me a favour?'

'Not by choice.'

'It's on behalf of Comisario Orifla.'

'That little bastard!'

'Find out, will you, when and why Señor Gaspari, who lives at Sa Serra, Meranitx, was granted permission to hold a revolver.'

'Give me time. The records are in a hell of a mess.'

Alvarez rang again just before lunch.

The assistant was resentful. 'Why the hell didn't you tell me the permission dated back to nineteen forty-four and then I could have told you it was impossible to check up on anything that far back.'

'Are you sure of that?'

'I'm bloody sure, mate, having spent hours searching through the old records that have bunged enough dust up my sinuses to strangle them.'

'Why was he granted a licence then?'

'Your guess is as good as mine. All the records show is that it was granted on the order of the Governor-General.'

'What?'

'No one less.'

Alvarez thanked the other, rang off. He fiddled with a pencil. The Governor-General, back in the days when his office granted him almost absolute power, would have concerned himself with the bureaucratic task of issuing a gun permit only in the most exceptional circumstances.

CHAPTER 10

The previous evening had shown him that just beyond the valley in which Sa Serra lay were two farms and it seemed reasonable to suppose that the occupants would know something about Gaspari. Initially, it proved to be a faulty supposition. The old man who lived in the first was partially deaf and wholly and ignorantly prejudiced—foreigners were evil and the only way of escaping their malign influence was to have absolutely nothing to do with them. If the devil drove into the valley every evening, he would not be surprised, but he would know nothing about it. The couple who worked the other farm were half his age and many times more intelligent; for them, foreigners represented the latest in agricultural techniques and machinery. Their land was as intensively cultivated as conditions allowed, their small herd of Holsteins were sleek, and their sheep and lambs were only distant cousins of the scraggy, wormy animals seen in many parts of the island.

Alvarez spoke about farming for a quarter of an hour, not only to create a rapport, but also because he was so interested in the subject; at the end of that time, he mentioned Gaspari.

'The Italian?' said the husband. Broad-shouldered, his face thickly featured, two days' growth of stubble on his chin, and wearing clothes fit for a scarecrow, he looked the traditional, small-minded peasant that he was not. 'We see him now and then.'

The wife had a cheerful face and a ready smile that disclosed two missing front teeth. 'But when you say do we know him well—he's not the man to stop and have a chat.'

'Not him!' agreed her husband. 'A couple of years back one of the sheep broke its hobble and went through into the valley and on to his land. You'd have thought it had knocked the house down, the way he carried on.'

'Has he lived here a long time?'

'He bought the place when my dad was alive—afore I was born, as a matter of fact. Dad always said he was a surly bastard, but not to get on the wrong side of him because he could mean big trouble.'

'D'you know what your father meant by that?'

'Not really.'

'What kind of visitors does he have these days?'

The husband looked puzzled. His wife said: 'How d'you mean, exactly?'

'Do they look wealthy? For instance, do they arrive in cars which make 'em seem the kind of people who don't know there's anything smaller than a ten-thousand-peseta note?'

'No one like that. Fact is, there's hardly anyone does visit him except the señor who turns up nearly every day and he's in just an ordinary car.'

'Then the señor's a bit of a hermit?'

'He's been that since his wife died. According to Elena, who works in the house, he's very secretive and sullen. But then, who's she to judge? She's not the best-tempered person on the island.'

'Think back over the past two or three weeks. Has there been a stranger around who seemed to be unusually interested in his place?'

'You're asking if maybe we saw whoever it was tried to break into the house?'

'That's right. It looks as if the burglar could have been here once before, spying out the lie of the land.'

She thought for a moment, looked at her husband who shook his head, said: 'The only stranger what's been around recently was the man a few days back.'

'Who was he?'

'He asked where Sa Serra was. Took a bit of understanding what he was after on account of him not speaking Spanish.'

'Can you describe him?'

She hesitated. 'That ain't going to be easy. I mean, he was in a car and didn't get out of it and I'd a goat that was doing poorly on a rope to see if the rough grass and weeds on the verge would help it.'

A vet's visit would probably have helped more, thought Alvarez; but although this couple were clearly relatively progressive in their farming, their attitude to money was the same as that of the most reactionary of peasants—they'd never spend a peseta unless the necessity of doing so could no longer be avoided. 'Just tell me as much about him as you can.'

'He'd a beard that was like a bramble patch and . . .'

It rapidly became clear that the beard was about the only physical feature of which she was certain. Yet it was her description of this that triggered Alvarez's memory and made him ask: 'Can you say what kind of a car he was driving?'

'Not really.'

He thanked them for their help, returned to his car and switched on the fan to clear the heat which had built up inside. A tumbleweed of a beard was a very weak peg on which to try to hang an identification. Yet this man might have been the same one who had been looking for Pedro.

His request was transmitted by the Centre of Communications in Palma to every office of the Cuerpo General de Policía on the island. Please ask car-hire firms to list anyone who has hired a car during the past two months for four weeks or longer. Then please check if the following description fitted any such hirer. Middle-aged, approximately one metre eighty tall, well built, brown hair with a touch of grey worn long, a luxuriant beard, and very blue eyes.

The inspector from Cala Forsaya rang on Tuesday morning. 'We've over two dozen firms in the area, but only one of 'em will handle long-term hirings because of the problems of insurance and servicing. They've four cars out for a month or more. One of the customers could fit the description. His name's Steven Armitage and the address he gave the car-hire firm is Hotel Trópico.'

'Is that actually in Cala Forsaya?'

'Yes, it is. I haven't checked that the señor is still booked in at the hotel, but he hasn't notified the car-hire firm that he's moved. D'you want me to make certain?'

'Thanks, but I reckon the best thing is for me to drive over. You won't mind if I move around in your territory without bothering you, will you?'

'Leave me in peace and you can take it over for all I give a damn.'

Once there had been fields, trees, sheep, goats, pigs, birds, space and solitude; now there was Cala Forsaya. Large hotels and blocks of apartments, restaurants, cafés, liquor and memento stores, lined and stretched back from the sandy beach.

Alvarez drove into the forecourt of the Hotel Trópico and parked. He stepped out into the blistering heat and walked across to the main entrance. The owner of the hotel clearly believed in character. The large foyer had potted plants and palms all over the place and a couple of caged macaws added jungle noises. Surprisingly, the two receptionists were not dressed in loincloths.

'Señor Armitage?' said the older of the receptionists. 'Yes, he's a guest.'

'Is he in at the moment?'

The receptionist studied the board. 'His key's not there so I'll try his room.' There was no answer to the telephone call. 'He's probably on the patio or the beach.'

On the beach side of the hotel there was a large, kidney-shaped pool which had a bar in the centre; almost all the bar stools, set in the water, were occupied, many by ladies whose only clothing was the briefest of monokinis. Alvarez enjoyed the attractive picture before regretfully concentrating on beards. There was none at the bar. The pool was surrounded by a tiled patio on which were a number of tables and chairs, each with a central sun umbrella. Almost all were occupied. At only one was there a beard and this was neatly trimmed and attached to an elderly man whose features bore the stern rectitude of an old-fashioned bishop for whom faith was a necessity, not an irrelevance.

He walked down to the beach. Here, there were two rows of 'Tahitian umbrellas' and by one sat a man with a very bushy beard and untidy long hair. When quite close, he looked up from the book he was reading and Alvarez was able to see the unusually deep blue eyes. He came to a stop. 'Señor Armitage?'

'And if I am?' The tone was more challenging than the words.

'My name is Inspector Alvarez, of the Cuerpo General de Policía. If it is convenient, I would like to talk to you.'

Facetiousness was the response of many when suddenly faced by a policeman. 'What's the problem? Have I parked on double yellow lines?'

'Quite frankly, I am not certain that you have done anything.'

'Then why do I have the pleasure?'

'I would like to know a little about your travels on the island.'

Armitage turned down the corner of a page, closed the paperback. 'Why should they interest you?'

'Would it be possible to move to somewhere cooler? I'm afraid I don't really enjoy the sun.'

'Will my room do? The walls are cracking, but the sun can't quite reach through them yet.' He looked at his watch. 'I do have an appointment later on, so the most I can give you is forty-five minutes. Since my travels have all been completely unexceptional, that should be time enough.'

His room on the fourth floor was large and it had two single beds and an en-suite bathroom; beyond the French window was a balcony with wrought-iron rails, which over-looked the sea.

He switched on a fan. 'This gives the illusion of coolness, if not the reality . . . Park yourself.' He indicated the chair that was by a small table on which was a holder containing several sheets of writing paper, envelopes, and group adver-tising brochures. 'Would you like a drink?'

'That would be very welcome, señor.'

'Not like the police at home! There's nothing like a teetotal policeman to make one feel guilty of every crime in the book and some that aren't yet even printed.'

'You sound experienced in such matters?'

'Not in the way you're now thinking. Two years ago the police showed an interest in me because I threw an overripe tomato at the Minister of Arts and missed the bastard of a Philistine—the only time I've regretted my uselessness at cricket. The inspector refused a drink with hypocritical mutterings about being on duty and so the PC with him had to go thirsty as well . . . The bar prices in this hotel are pitched at the Gettys of the world, so I keep my own stock up here. Limited choice, but unlimited quantity.' He crossed to the built-in cupboard by the left of the bathroom door, opened this, and brought out two glasses and a Thermos flask. He tapped the flask. 'The chambermaid has a squint, but ever since I told her that she'd a magnificent facial bone structure, she's kept me supplied with ice. I can offer you gin, whisky, or brandy, together with soda, tonic or water.'

'May I have a coñac with just ice, please?'

He produced a bottle of Soberano and poured two large drinks, added three ice cubes to each. 'According to an acquaintance, it's only men with hair on their chests who drink brandy.'

He was playing a part, thought Alvarez; the breezy extrovert who couldn't help being a bit of a clown. Playing it because he always did or because he had something serious to conceal?

Armitage crossed to hand him a glass, then went over to one of the beds and sprawled out on that. 'So you say you're interested in my journeyings. Why?'

'I think that will become clear, señor. How long have you been staying in this hotel?'

'That really is relevant?' He shrugged his shoulders. 'I suppose it's getting on towards a couple of months.'

'That's a long time.'

'In whose terms?'

'When compared to the average tourist. Perhaps you have a definite reason for being here?'

'Three definite reasons: the sun, the sea, and the wine. The fourth requirement for the perfect summer holiday, sex, naturally doesn't concern me at my age.'

Alvarez had to smile at that barefaced lie; Armitage's face spoke unmistakably of an actively libidinous nature. 'There is not a further reason?'

'No.'

'Then you do not have a job in England?'

'I am a sculptor and therefore am lucky in that my time is my own. I am unlucky in that I possess a certain amount of natural talent.'

'I do not quite understand that.'

'Then you know nothing of modern sculpture and the dust-bowl minds of those who award prizes in competitions.'

'In the weeks you have been here, have you travelled about the island?'

'I've been to most places that the tourists ignore.'

'Have you had any definite objective for your travels?'

'Merely idle, but never patronizing, curiosity.'

'Have you ever been to Puerto Llueso?'

Armitage drained his glass, slid off the bed and walked over to the cupboard. As he refilled his glass, he said: 'I don't recognize the name.'

'It's on the north-east coast. If you have ever visited the Parelona peninsula, you must have passed through it.'

'Then I have, because I once set out to go to Parelona beach on the recommendation of the concierge. He said it was the most beautiful in the world. When I saw rows of tourist buses in the car park, I left without bothering to find out if his judgement was just.'

'Did you stop in Puerto Llueso?'

'I certainly don't remember doing so.' He returned to the bed.

'Have you ever been to Meranitx?'

'Where's that?'

'In the mountains, to the north-west.'

'I've spent a lot of time in the mountains because they're empty of people and I'm fascinated by the way in which different light alters their forms, but I'm fairly certain I've never been to the place you've just mentioned.'

'Have you ever met a man known as Pedro the Simple; or Pedro the Iceman?'

'That sounds like Happy Families; Mr Bun the baker. No, I've not met Pedro, by any name.'

'He's an old man who, in the days when ordinary people did not have refrigerators, made a living from selling ice.'

'Not the kind of person I'd be likely to meet. And I hasten to add that I don't say that from any snobbish reason. But as a tourist who speaks no Mallorquin, I find it quite impossible to make contact with the ordinary person.'

'How did you know that he spoke only Mallorquin, not Castilian?'

'Someone here in the hotel told me that many of the elderly speak only Mallorquin. You said he was old, so I just presumed.' He stood. 'Your glass has been empty for quite some time; a grave social solecism on my part.'

Alvarez put his next question after he'd been handed back his refilled glass. 'About ten days ago, did you drive to Maranitx?'

'I thought we'd covered that question?'

'And while there, did you speak to a couple and ask them where Sa Serra was?'

'I'd say it's about time you explained what all this is in aid of.'

'Pedro the Simple—or Pedro the Iceman—has been killed.'

'He . . .'

'The news of his death concerns you?'

'Any man's death diminishes me.'

'I beg your pardon?'

'We British are taught that it's the Donne thing always to be concerned by another's death; provided, of course, that such concern doesn't inconvenience one.'

'He fell to his death and it may not have been an accident. Early on Friday morning, someone tried to break into Sa Serra, but stopped when the alarm sounded.'

'On this lotus island, I imagine you call this a crime wave?'

'Can you tell me anything about Pedro's death or the attempted break-in?'

'Nothing at all.'

'If you do know something about either, or both, it would make things easier if you say so now.'

'I always find it difficult to admit to an actual transgression; I find it impossible to admit to an imagined one.'

'Then I must ask you to come with me.'

'To where?'

'Puerto Llueso and Maranitx. Then I can discover whether you have been telling me the truth.'

'How can the proposed jaunt do that?'

'It will show whether you are the man who asked the English señora if she could tell him where Pedro the Iceman lived; and who asked a couple near Sa Serra where that property was.'

Armitage stood and went over to the French window and stared out. 'The other day I was told that here in Spain you have the expression, an Englishman's word. I give you my English word that I know nothing about the death.'

'Unfortunately, señor, since tourism has brought so many English to the island, the expression no longer has any currency. Will you please come with me now.'

'I told you, I have an appointment.'

'I suggest you telephone the person concerned and explain that you will be rather late.'

Armitage swung round, his expression bitterly angry. He crossed to the telephone, which was on the table between the beds, lifted the receiver, spoke to the member of staff who was operating the switchboard and asked for ninety-one, forty-six, twelve zero. The connection was soon made. 'Nicola, it's Steve. Look, I'm very sorry, but something's cropped up and I won't be able to make your place on time . . . No, just totally unexpected . . . Quite certain . . . I'll give you all the details when I see you.' He rang off.

'If we travel in two cars,' said Alvarez, 'we can go our own ways afterwards.'

'Aren't you worried I might take off in the opposite direction to you?'

'Why should you, señor, when neither Pedro's death nor the attempted break-in in any way concerns you? In any case, this is a small island and one cannot drive very far in the opposite direction to anywhere.'

CHAPTER 11

They parked in front of the bungalow at the back of Puerto Llueso and as they climbed out of their cars, they could hear children screaming. 'The señora has three small children,' said Alvarez.

Armitage, now dressed in cotton shirt and shorts, muttered: 'It sounds more like a dozen.'

They walked up the path through the front garden—garden only in name—to the front door. Alvarez rang the bell. Armitage turned round to face the bay. Angela Dominguez opened the door and said in flustered Spanish: 'What is it?'

'I'm sorry to have to bother you at such a time,' replied Alvarez in English.

'It's not really as bad as it sounds . . . Oh, it's you!'

Eulalia appeared in the hall, thumb in mouth. Alvarez waved at her. She stared at him for several seconds, then rushed back the way she had come. There was the sound of a crash and this was followed by fresh screaming.

'Oh my God, now what?' Angela disappeared.

After a while the screaming died away and she reappeared with one of the twins in her arms. 'Eulalia ran into him . . . For heaven's sake, come inside instead of standing out in the boiling sun. I'll make some coffee.'

'Thank you, señora, but we certainly aren't going to cause you so much trouble. All I wish is to ask you if you have seen the señor before. Then we will leave you in peace.'

'More like in pieces.'

He smiled. He said to Armitage: 'Please turn round, señor.'

Armitage hesitated, then swung round.

She said without any hesitation: 'He's the man I told you asked me if I knew where Pedro lived. I couldn't mistake that beard . . .' She became silent as she realized the possible significance of her identification.

'Thank you, señora. We need disturb you no longer.'

Alvarez walked back up the weed-covered path, opened the front gate, and waited by the side of his car. Armitage came to a stop and said bitterly: 'I should have remembered to shave off my beard or, at the very least, trim it.'

'I think it might look better trimmed . . . Do you now admit that you are the man who asked the señora where Pedro the Iceman lived?'

'There's hardly any point in my trying to deny it.'

'You knew Pedro Segui?'

'No.'

'Then why did you wish to discover where he lived?'

'I did not kill him.'

'Were you with him when he died?'

'No.'

Alvarez took a handkerchief from his pocket and wiped the sweat from his forehead, face, and neck. 'It is very hot here. I suggest we drive down to the port and find a bar where they do not charge tourist prices and where it will be so much more pleasant for you to explain everything.'

'I thought it was your job to make things as unpleasant as possible for other people? You seem to be the strangest goddamn policeman!'

The owner of the bar did not actively discourage tourists— no Mallorquin ever discouraged profit—but he did not actively encourage them by redecorating and putting up welcoming notices in English. The bar was dark, the walls were bare of gimmicky decorations, the wooden tables had no beer mats on them, and drinks were still served with some of the locally cured, bitter olives at no extra charge.

While Armitage sat at one of the corner tables, Alvarez went over to the bar. 'So how's life?'

'It was all right until a moment ago,' replied the owner.

'What's the problem—a guilty conscience? Been buying smuggled fags again?'

'Never touch 'em.'

'That's not how I hear things.'

'Then you've got twisted hearing, like every other bloody copper . . . What d'you want?'

'Two coffees and two coñacs.'

'Are you paying for them?'

'Don't I always?'

'Are you trying to get me to laugh?' But, satisfied he was not going to have to provide free drinks for two, he became more cheerful.

Alvarez carried the coffees, brandies, and an earthenware bowl of olives over to the corner table. 'The olives are perhaps an acquired taste, señor, but will you try one?'

'Not if it's anything like the one I had the other day. Wormwood soaked in gall.'

Alvarez ate an olive, dropped the stone into an ashtray. 'Why did you wish to meet Pedro?'

'Does it matter?'

'Very much.'

'Suppose I tell you I've forgotten?'

'You are too intelligent to make such an answer. After all, if you had nothing to do with his death, you can have no reason for not telling me why you sought him out.'

'The logic of the policeman who thinks everything has to be either black or white. Life's about shades of grey.'

'Which, señor, is why we are sitting here and not in some hot and smelly interview room.'

'Point taken.' Armitage drank, put the glass down. 'What kind of relationship did you have with your father? A good one?'

'But of course.'

'It still comes naturally out here to answer "of course", doesn't it? Not back home, not even when I was a kid. One was expected to be at odds because he was bound to be so antediluvian and out-of-touch with real life. Since I never knew mine, I couldn't row with him. So he's always occupied the high ground with his head somewhere up with the clouds.' There was a touch of resentment in his voice, as if he would have preferred a father slightly less perfect. After a moment, he slowly described all that had happened to bring him out to the island.

At the conclusion of his story Alvarez picked up the two glasses and took them over to the bar to be refilled, then returned to the table and sat. 'You were convinced that if the Pedro in the photograph turned out to be the Pedro to whom your father had spoken, all you had ever been told about his death was wrong.'

'Part of it had to be; perhaps all of it was. But more importantly for me, if Pedro was the same man, then that letter was written to my mother and she had kept it because of love, not hate.'

'What could Pedro tell you?'

Armitage fiddled with the glass, twisting it round, his deep blue eyes unfocused. 'The first meeting was farcical. I don't speak Spanish so I took along a dictionary, hoping that that would enable us to communicate. Nobody then had told me that a lot of the older people couldn't read or write and only spoke Mallorquin. I talked to him in dictionary Spanish, he replied in Mallorquin, and if we both understood a single word, I'm damned if I know what that was.

'Obviously, I needed an interpreter. So I persuaded one of the waiters at the hotel who spoke a kind of American gangster English to go along with me on a second visit. It was a stupid choice. He was a smart Alec and contemptuous of everyone and everything from the past. Sixty seconds after meeting Pedro he was treating him with rude contempt. Instead of becoming angry, Pedro became frightened and in the end he took off at a rate of knots and disappeared in the rough land at the back of his shack. We waited, but he didn't return. When we were back at the hotel, the waiter tried to take me for twice what I'd agreed to pay on the grounds that Pedro was a complete idiot.

'I went back on my own, for the third time, with a Mallorquin dictionary, but there was no sign of Pedro. I hung on for a bit, but I gained the impression he was somewhere nearby and watching and wasn't going to show while I was around.'

'On your second visit, were you able to learn anything before he ran away?'

'I think so, only it was impossible to be certain. The waiter said Pedro would only talk about the price of ice and I couldn't get the stupid young oaf to try to find out why that obviously meant a lot to Pedro. It was my guess that in some way that anchored the past for him.

'Still, one of the things that did come out was that Pedro had met my father twice—he could be certain of that because the second time the ice-making machine was always breaking down. The importance of that is that as far as I know, my father had only once been on the island, on his honeymoon. So here was confirmation of the possibility that he had been here in 'forty-two.'

'Have you any idea why the official version of his death may have been falsified?'

'None. But assuming that it was, then the falsification must have been carried out at a very high level. My mother's pension was considerably more than she could normally have expected and only someone way up on the power ladder could have arranged that.'

'Do you imagine that she realized her pension was un-usually generous?'

'She was a very intelligent woman, so she must have done. And she must also have seen that this was in the nature of a bribe to keep her mouth shut—she knew from the letter that the official version of events had to be wrong. Had she been on her own, I haven't the slightest doubt she would never have accepted it, but would have forced the truth out into the open because she believed that truth was the second most important thing in the world. But I was the most important and she needed as much money as she could lay her hands on in order to bring me up in the way she wanted to.'

'Do you have the letter here?'

'It was stolen. Stupidly—maybe it was a gesture of temporary rejection—I returned it to the secret compartment in the desk. When I went to retrieve it, it had gone.'

'The house had been burgled?'

'Nothing else was missing, not even an envelope in the same compartment in which was a block of four stamps that is worth the right side of twenty thousand pounds.'

'Who knew about this letter?'

'Only a couple of people.'

'Was either in a position of authority?'

'One almost certainly was.'

'Did you report the theft to the police?'

'Yes. And they couldn't have been less interested.'

'Did you not explain the significance of it to them?'

'In very general terms, but it didn't make any difference. There are so many burglaries these days that unless you lose a couple of Gauguins, the police shrug their shoulders.'

Alvarez drained his cup. He brought a pack of cigarettes from his pocket. 'Do you smoke?'

'Cheroots only and I've managed to keep off them for quite some time now.'

He lit a cigarette. 'When you were talking to Pedro, were you able to learn anything that could explain why your father might have been on the island a second time?'

'I thought for a bit I had, but later on I came to the conclusion that the waiter had been right and it was just more of Pedro's stupidities.'

'What was this?'

'Pedro talked about Bassa Gris—the waiter told me that that's a local army base. I wanted to find out if Pedro was trying to suggest my father was somehow connected with the base, but pretty soon after he mentioned it was when he became so frightened he ran off.'

'You don't now believe there could have been a connection?'

'Father was a serving naval officer, so he must have been in mufti. If anyone in authority had identified him, he'd have been arrested double quick sharp. So common sense says he'd have kept as far away from danger spots as possible.'

'Even so, you did nothing to check the possibility?'

'As a matter of fact . . . It probably seems bloody stupid now, having just explained why it had to be so unlikely, but it occurred to me that because it was so unlikely, it might just be possible. The whole affair, logically speaking, was so crazy that anything illogical became possible. That won't make sense to you.'

'I think I understand.'

'Then you must have a mind as crooked as mine.' Armitage grimaced. 'That was a poor choice of words.'

'I understand you mean a mind capable of thinking along twisting paths, not one which is criminally inclined . . . Will you have another coñac, señor?'

'Yeah, only this time I shout.' He picked up the glasses and went over to the bar. When he returned, he said: 'I heard that the cost of living here is slightly more than it is back home, but all the while I can buy a brandy for a hundred and fifty pesetas I reckon that that's nonsense.'

'How much?'

'A hundred and fifty. Why?'

'Excuse me.' Alvarez stood and crossed to the bar. 'Beltrán.'

The owner moved along the bar. 'Yeah?'

'I think you've made a small mistake.'

'Letting a policeman in here is a big mistake, not a small one.'

'Asking a hundred and fifty pesetas for a hundred-peseta brandy is an even bigger one.'

'Tourist brandy is a hundred and fifty.'

'Which has just gone through the till so that it is on record for the income tax and the IVA man who wish to assess your true profits as opposed to the ones you declare?'

Mallorquin was a useful language in which to swear because there were no recognized limits of bad taste. Still muttering, the owner went over to the till and took out a hundred-peseta coin which he slapped down on the bar. 'Tell him not to spend it all at once.' His tone expressed anger, admiration and scorn; anger that he had lost a hundred pesetas, admiration for Alvarez's cupidity, and scorn that such cupidity should be put to the advantage of a foreigner.

Back at the table and after he'd passed over the hundred pesetas, Alvarez said: 'Did you visit Bassa Gris?'

'I went along one day. There were a couple of armed guards at the barrier with whom I tried to communicate and in the end they called up a lieutenant who spoke darned good English. He told me his name was Pons and he made a very laboured pun on *pons asinorum* and how that was so suitable for him since he was in charge of recruits ... I explained what I wanted and he agreed to do what he could to help. He left me in a room after giving me some magazines to look through and apologizing profusely because they weren't in English. When he returned he said he hadn't been able to have a word with the chap he'd wanted to because the other was off until the next day, but he had managed to speak to someone who'd been around a long time. This bloke could just remember the days when a man who was simple had come out from the port three times a week with a donkey to sell ice—that had to be Pedro. Pons suggested I returned the next afternoon by which time he should have managed to have a word with the other chap.

'I returned and at the barrier asked for Pons. The results were very different from what I'd expected. An armed guard marched me into an office and the colonel—a beady man with a beady eye—told me in disjointed but recognizable English that Lieutenant Pons was away, the base was under the tightest security, people who asked questions concerning it were liable to be identified as spies, and spies were shot. He suggested I got the hell out of it.'

'Army colonels are notorious for having very large tempers and very small minds. So what did you do next?'

'I didn't do anything. I wasn't going to get anywhere at the base, unless to my own funeral, and I'd proved to my own satisfaction that the letter had been written to my mother. That was that.'

'But you had not learned why your father had been on the island and why he might have visited the base?'

'The older you get, the more easily you accept that there aren't answers to all the questions.'

'You were not still sufficiently curious to want to discover the truth?'

'Not really.'

'Yet you have stayed on the island?'

'It's like Aeaea—once you've landed, you lose all desire to leave. Not, I hope, that I've been turned into a swine.'

'If you had decided not to pursue your inquiries, why did you wish to know where Señor Gaspari lives?'

'Who?'

'Recently, someone tried to break into his house. Yet it seems he owns little worth stealing.'

'Obviously the intruder thought differently.'

'Señor, did you not speak to the señora who farms the land beyond the valley in which lies Sa Serra and did you not ask her where exactly was Señor Gaspari's house?'

'I did not.'

'It is too late to drive there now, but tomorrow you will accompany me and we will discover whether she recognizes you.'

'Which she won't, unless she's lying.'

'Right now, I think it is you who lies. A man only lies when he has cause.'

'A profound statement that isn't true. I know someone who lies all the time because it amuses him to discover how gullible people are.'

'The consequences of lying to the police are often far from amusing.'

'Another profound statement and one with which I feel it's better not to argue.'

Alvarez finished his drink. 'Before we separate, I must ask you to give me several of the hairs from your head and from your beard.'

'Obviously for comparison, but with what?' Armitage

appeared to stare deeply into his glass, as if for him it was a crystal ball. 'I presume, with the hairs you say you found on Pedro. In which case, you may have as many as you like since hair is one of the few things I possess in abundance.'

There could be no mistaking the careless confidence with which he had spoken.

CHAPTER 12

Soon after leaving the café, Alvarez turned off the road into the forecourt of the petrol station which was on the outskirts of the port. He braked to a halt behind two other cars that were waiting to be served, leaned back, and thought about what he had just learned. He judged that Armitage had been both telling the truth and lying; the truth about his meetings with Pedro, his trip to the army base, and his denial that he had been present at Pedro's death, lies when he claimed it had not been he who had asked directions to Sa Serra or who had later attempted to break into the house.

Why had he lied? Two answers immediately suggested themselves. He could judge that the identification of him must have been a poor one and therefore easily challenged; clearly, if he admitted to being the man who had asked where was Sa Serra, it became very likely that it had been he who had attempted to break in . . .

'D'you want petrol or are you here for the rest?' asked one of the attendants.

Alvarez drove forward, switched off the engine, and handed the key to the petrol cap through the opened window. 'A thousand pesetas' worth. And I'll be watching the meter.'

'You mean to say you can read?'

Three minutes later, and after a brief wait for oncoming traffic to clear, he drew out of the forecourt and drove towards Llueso. Until now, only one thing had connected

Pedro's death with the attempted break-in at Sa Serra—
the wife's description of the man in the car. Armitage denied
the description and the wife would probably withdraw it
if strongly challenged. Assuming Armitage had not been
present at Pedro's death, then what possible motive could
there be for his trying to break into Sa Serra? So had the
man with the beard been Armitage? Had he been Armitage,
but the burglar had been someone else? If so, why would
Armitage deny it had been he who had been in the car? The
burglar must have surveyed Sa Serra to know he was going
to have to break through glass, which suggested criminal
experience; but the fact that, having forced the shutter, he
had not made any search for an alarm spoke of a rank
amateur . . . This contradiction could be resolved if one
cast Armitage as the intruder with a motive strong enough
to make him sufficiently determined to reconnoitre the
property first. But it was a lack of motive which so strongly
militated against his guilt . . .

He suddenly realized something. Use considerable imagination and there was a second factor to connect Pedro's
death with the attempted break-in: the wrongful use of
power.

Assume that Armitage's father had been on the island in
'forty-two, then the official version of his death had to be
wrong. Only people with very great power and authority
could have commissioned such a lie. The letter Armitage
had found was proof, to those who could read what it really
said, that the official version of the death had to be a lie.
Only people of power and authority could organize the theft
of such proof. To turn to events on the island. Superior
Chief Salas had ordered him to make inquiries into the
attempted break-in—even though Gaspari was a foreigner,
normally he would not have expected to be seconded to so
minor a case. Then did Gaspari have some special pull with
authority? The preliminary inquiry had turned up questions
which should have been answered. Yet even before he'd had
time to report to Salas, Commisario Orifla had been placed

in charge of the case and had ordered him to close his investigations. Orifla would not, solely on his own authority, ever have shut down the case so prematurely, so he must have been told to do so by Salas. Salas was a man who never moved forward without making absolutely certain that his back was covered. He would not have taken the risk of groundlessly stopping the investigation unless he had an order from high authority to cover him should his decision be challenged . . .

Accept that the two cases were linked by an abuse of power. Then what could have happened nearly fifty years ago to warrant such abuse? . . . If he had a gramme of common sense, he'd forget everything and not pursue the problem. If there were one incontrovertible fact of life, it was that while the pursuit of truth was the noblest of causes, it could also be a fatal one. Truth was small counterweight to power.

Dolores looked across the table. 'Enrique, you're not eating properly.'

'What's that?' Alvarez jerked his mind back from the problems which were so occupying him.

'You're hardly touching your food.' There was annoyance as well as concern in her voice.

'That's only because I was thinking.' He hurriedly resumed eating the frito Mallorquin. There was no quicker way of provoking her bad temper than to criticize, either directly or by inference, her cooking.

'It seems these days you've a lot on your mind,' said Jaime.

'Which is more than anyone's ever been able to say about you,' she snapped. She turned. 'Are you sure you're feeling all right, Enrique?'

'I'm fine.'

'Can't you see that he's counting orange trees?' said Jaime.

'You've drunk too much again.'

'I had one small coñac before the meal and just one glass of wine so far with it.'

'You had two large coñacs,' Juan piped up, 'and that's your third glass of wine.'

Jaime looked at his son and considered a good clip around the ears—out of sight of Dolores.

'I've been too concerned about Enrique to watch,' she confessed with annoyance.

'I keep telling you, nothing's wrong,' said Alvarez. He was going to have to ask for a second helping of frito.

'All I'm saying is—' began Jaime.

'Why can you not remember that for you, silence is advisable?'

'Oh, it is, is it? I go out and earn all the money that pays for the food—'

'You are the only one who works? Does no one have to go shopping every day and stand in queues for hours? Does no one have to cook in a kitchen that is so hot it would melt a stony heart? You wouldn't know. You are a man, so you demand food when you want it and never concern yourself with the suffering of the person who has to slave in order that you can overfill your gross belly.'

'Sweet Mary! All I was saying was that Enrique was counting orange trees—'

Juan, unable to follow the logic of the conversation, said: 'But he hasn't got any orange trees.'

'Exactly!' snapped Dolores.

Jaime leaned forward until his stomach was hard up against the table. 'Come on, tell me—what's so stupid about it?'

'Cousin Francisca is a woman of feeling and taste.'

Juan became even more mystified, but a quick look at his mother's expression suggested he should not try to elucidate the problem.

Alvarez slumped back in the chair in his office and stared out through the opened and unshuttered window as he considered yet again all the facts he knew or surmised.

Then he sat upright, checked the number in the telephone directory, dialled it. When the connection was made, he identified himself. 'I'd be grateful if you'll identify a number for me. It's ninety-one—'

The woman interrupted him. 'That's not the business of this department.'

'The last time I needed a number identified, I checked with management and they said that it was.'

There was a pause. 'We're very busy, so call back tomorrow.'

'It is priority so perhaps you'll check it out right away and ring me back?'

'You seem to think we've nothing else to do.'

He gave her the number, thanked her for her help, rang off. There was considerable satisfaction to be gained from knowing that for once he had got the better of one of the notoriously rude telephone employees.

He dialled the forensic laboratory in Palma and spoke to one of the assistants. 'I've another sample of hair which I'll send in by bus this morning. Will you arrange for someone to collect it from the station and then compare it with the incident hairs you have?'

'What's the reference?'

'It's the Pedro Segui case.'

'Hang on.'

He waited. He hadn't the slightest doubt that the tests would indicate that Armitage's hairs did not match those which had been caught up in Pedro's nail . . .

'I've checked and we don't have the hairs any longer.'

'But they were to be held by you in case I decided to get permission to have a DNA job done in Madrid.'

'I wouldn't know anything about that.'

'What have you done with them?'

'Returned them to you, of course.'

'When?'

'At the end of last week, according to the records.'

'Nothing's arrived.'

'Then there's been some sort of a hang-up.' The speaker did not sound surprised.

'Who collected them?'

'How would I know?'

'Could you try and find out—it's important?'

'All right,' agreed the other reluctantly.

The two calls came within minutes of each other. The first was from the forensic lab.

'I've found out as much as I can. The order to pack up the hairs and return them came from the superior chief's office. No one seems to know who the man was who collected them.'

'Surely he had to sign for them?' asked Alvarez.

'Yeah. But I've had a look at the signature and if you can make anything of it, you're a genius.'

'Who handed them over?'

'One of the secretaries.'

'Can't she identify the man?'

'Never clapped eyes on him before and her description doesn't fit anyone I know.'

'If she couldn't identify him, how could she be certain he was authorized to receive them?'

'He asked for them.'

It was a logic which Alvarez would normally have accepted, but in this instance it made him swear. 'Doesn't she know the rules say she should have checked his authority before handing over anything?'

'And don't you know how things work in practice?'

He asked the other to make certain that the third sample of hairs should not be handed over to anyone without his direct authorization, rang off.

The second call came within seconds. 'That number you asked me to trace belongs to Señor Scalfaro.'

'Well I'll be damned!' he said. 'Is his christian name Fermo?'

'That's right.'

'Can you give me the address?'

'Ca Na Florina, Biniarch; there's no road listed.'

He replaced the receiver. The woman with whom Armitage had had a date lived with, or at least was connected with, Scalfaro, who had been at Gaspari's house. Here, surely, was evidence that there was a direct connection between Pedro and the attempted break-in at Sa Serra and therefore proof that Armitage had continued to lie?

He lifted the receiver and dialled Salas's number. The plum-voiced secretary answered the call and told him the superior chief was not in the office and wouldn't be for the rest of the day.

'Maybe you can help me? I'm wondering why the superior chief gave orders for the two samples of hair from the Segui case to be returned to me?'

'He has given no such orders.'

'How certain of that can you be?'

'I do not make a statement if I am not certain of the facts,' she replied with chilling hauteur.

'Could someone have given the order, using his name, but without his being aware of the fact?'

'Who would dare do such a thing?'

Who indeed?

He replaced the receiver. The hairs had been collected from the laboratory, but had not been returned to him. Things on the island moved slowly, but not that slowly. Those hairs had disappeared for good and any investigation into their disappearance would come to the inevitable conclusion that somewhere along the line there had been sloppy inefficiency but, since the person concerned was most unlikely to be identified, there was no point in pursuing the matter. Yet he was certain this was not a case of inefficiency, there had been a deliberate destruction of evidence in order to pervert the course of justice. And that had been ordered by someone very high up . . .

There was an old Mallorquin saying. When the genet's abroad, a mouse's only chance of survival is to hide.

CHAPTER 13

Biniarch was a village of narrow, twisting streets, two small squares, and one large church, set on and about a hill which overlooked the central plain. Many years before, it had been noted for its lace, but now only a few elderly women still carried out such work and all attempts to interest younger women in learning the traditional skills had failed so that it seemed certain the craft would be lost. The village lay on the way to nowhere and few tourists ever bothered to visit it, in consequence it had escaped the results of the crass commercialism which had overtaken and submerged so many other places; indirectly, and perhaps ironically, however, its present prosperity was entirely due to the tourists— the villagers owned land on the plain which was rich and blessed with plentiful water and they grew large quantities of fruit and vegetables; produce which now sold for so much money that the older and more unsophisticated among them were fearful.

Alvarez was directed to a dirt track a kilometre from the village, which wound its way eastwards along the side of the hill. Ca Na Florina lay at the end of this. It was a small, traditional Mallorquin farmhouse, in good repair and in appearance unaltered. The land about it was terraced and since this grew citrus fruit, loquats and olives, and there was no readily discernible garden, it was not immediately apparent that the property was owned by a foreigner; one needed the sharp eyes of a Mallorquin peasant to discern from the absence of any sheep, goats, pigs or pigeons, that it was.

He left his car by the side of a lean-to garage, the rear of which was the stone wall of the terrace immediately behind the house, and walked along to the front door that had the traditional cat hole in the bottom right-hand corner.

Because the house was owned by a foreigner, he knocked and waited, instead of stepping inside and calling out.

The door was opened by a woman who, as far as he could judge—which, as for most men, was not very far—was about his own age. She was not in any sense beautiful, having irregular and at times heavy features, but her looks attracted attention and, once he was attracted, an onlooker began to appreciate that behind her sophistication—evidenced by the clothes she wore and her make-up—she was a woman of considerable intelligence and with a warm nature. This last judgement was reinforced whenever she smiled.

He introduced himself. 'Is it possible to speak with Señor Scalfaro?' he asked.

Showing only mild curiosity, she asked him inside, her Spanish accentless.

The first room was an entrance hall which did not double as a formal reception room as it probably would have done had the house been owned by a Mallorquin. The furnishings were simple; flamed prints hung on the walls, the large fireplace was not used and fixed on the inside walls were ancient iron and brass kitchen utensils, there was a bookcase filled to capacity, an aspidistra in a brass cauldron, two matching, antique Mallorquin tables, and a carpet on the tiled floor.

'My father's through here,' she said.

The sitting-room was furnished equally simply, with a couple of antique cupboards and a spinning wheel, which looked as if it might still be in use, to add character. A television in the far corner was showing a programme in Italian.

'Father, this is Inspector Alvarez of—' she began.

'Of the Cuerpo General de Policía,' completed Scalfaro, as he stood and switched off the television by remote control.

'You've already met?'

'At Gio's, when the Inspector was inquiring into that burglary that wasn't quite.' He came forward and shook hands with Alvarez. 'Please sit down. And let me offer you a drink. What would you like?'

'May I have a coñac, with just ice, please?' Alvarez settled on a very comfortable armchair.

'I'll get it,' she said. 'And presumably you'll have your usual?'

'Of course. As you said the other day in some exasperation, I am a man of inflexible routine.' As she left, he said to Alvarez: 'My favourite drink is Campari and orange juice with a touch of bitters. A very Italian drink, it was once described as; since the speaker was an Austrian, I imagine the inference was a derogatory one.' He sat. 'I presume we owe the pleasure of your visit to that attempted break-in— have you managed to identify the would-be thief?'

'Unfortunately, not yet, señor.'

'And you think I may be able to help you?'

'I hope so. Have you known Señor Gaspari for a long time?'

'As a matter of fact I have, yes.'

'Before nineteen forty-four?'

Scalfaro looked quizzically at him. 'Is that a date plucked out of the air or do you have a reason for naming it?'

'It's when the señor was first issued with permission to keep a revolver.'

'As long ago as that?'

'The permission was granted on the order of the Governor-General. That's so unusual that I've been wondering whether he knew him personally. Did you also know the Governor-General personally?'

'Did I say I was on the island at that time?'

'I'm sorry, I should have asked you that first. I'm afraid I do get muddled.'

'Inspector, I am more than ready to help you as far as I can, but I don't think I'm being unreasonable if I say that I would like to see some relevance to your questions.'

'Suppose I assure you that they are relevant?'

Scalfaro looked perplexed. His daughter returned, a tray in her right hand. She handed a glass to Alvarez, one to her father, and kept the third for herself. She sat on the settee, every movement graceful. As soon as she was settled, she said to her father: 'Is something wrong?'

'Not really,' he answered. 'It's merely that I'm finding it difficult to understand why the Inspector's interested in whether or not I knew the Governor-General fifty years ago.'

'What on earth can that have to do with the burglary?'

'Precisely the point which intrigues me.'

'Señor,' said Alvarez, 'I cannot answer you because I don't know.'

'I must commend you on such honesty! Most policemen, in my very limited experience, like to claim omniscience. Your baffled uncertainty comes as a breath of fresh air.'

That could have been said sneeringly, but Scalfaro's tone had made his words a shared joke. 'If the truth is ever told, most policemen for most of the time and in most of their cases are as uncertain as I am now.'

'Then let's lessen your uncertainty as far as we can. I did live here in 'forty-four, but I did not know anyone even half as grand as the Governor-General.'

'Very few foreigners settled here in those days.'

'I presume that's an observation and not a question?'

'I don't really know.'

'More uncertainty? I think it's likely you're really asking me what I was doing here at such a time but, with commendable tact, you don't like to put the question that baldly in case it causes me embarrassment.' His tone was light. 'The facts are simple. I was in the Italian navy in a lowly position and in the course of such service I contracted TB. After some time in hospital I was discharged from there and— when it was decided I still wasn't fit enough to go out and be killed—from the navy. This island had suffered during the Civil War, but in 'forty-four it knew peace and a certain detachment from the world's ills. I wangled permission to come here for a recuperative rest, saw, and was conquered by its beauty. I've never regretted my flight from harsh reality.'

'And your wife came with you?'

'Sadly, my first wife had died earlier—which was a further reason for running away. I once read that life is a sadistic joker. I'd sent her into the country for safety, to stay with relatives who farmed in the middle of nowhere and had never heard an explosion in anger. She tripped as she climbed out of a tin bath, fractured her skull on a shelf, and died.

'Here, I married a second time to a Mallorquin. We lived happily ever after—that is, until she died a couple of years ago. Nicola was born in this house. Sadly, she also has had to learn just how sadistic a joker life can be—'

'The Inspector won't want to hear about me,' she said sharply.

'I was under the impression that he wanted to hear about everything, however seemingly irrelevant, since he has no idea what is and what is not important.'

'You realize you sound very rude?'

Scalfaro said to Alvarez: 'Like any well-brought-up, modern Italian daughter, Nicola is very quick to point out to her father his many faults. I must apologize if I've sounded rude. Regrettably, I often tend to become facetious when I meet someone with whom I feel an instinctive compatibility. I don't know why.'

'Because you're jockeying for position,' she said, 'in a typical male attempt to claim the high ground.'

'What absolute rubbish! What a pity that modern woman has learned less than nothing about modern man . . . Inspector, your glass is empty. You will allow me to refill it?'

She stood. 'I'll do it.'

'Admirable, dutiful daughter!'

Scalfaro watched her leave the room, then turned back. 'There are times when, though far from a bitter woman, she appears bitter. That is because she has known great unhappiness. Her husband suffered a heart attack that killed him within fifteen minutes. Doubly unfortunately, it occurred in another woman's bed. Life, ever the sadistic joker. Perhaps it is stupid of me, but I hope that maybe life will relent for her and she will find happiness once more.'

'With Steven Armitage?'

Scalfaro stared at Alvarez. 'How do you know about their relationship?'

'I've had reason to speak to Señor Armitage on several occasions and in the course of one he needed to telephone a lady to delay the appointment he had with her. It was made from a hotel and he had to ask the hotel switchboard operator to obtain the number. That proved to be the number of this house.'

'Clearly, you don't miss much. Not exactly the slightly bewildered country policeman you'd have the world believe.'

'I'm often very bewildered.'

'And perhaps slightly devious? Have we finally reached the true reason for your visit? Yet what can the relationship existing between Nicola and Steven possibly have to do with the attempted break-in at Sa Serra?'

'One more question to which I have no answer.'

'I no longer accept your disarming confessions because now I can sense the cunning of simplicity.'

'I'm not quite certain what that means.'

'You confirm my suspicions.'

Nicola returned, handed Alvarez his refilled glass, settled once more on the settee. Scalfaro said to her: 'The Inspector knows Steven.'

'Yes.'

'The news doesn't surprise you?'

'Steve told me.'

'Then why didn't you, in good time, tell me?'

'It seemed completely unimportant.'

'You will have to learn to judge more accurately. I suspect

that in the eyes of the Inspector, your friendship with Steven is of the greatest importance and the reason he is here now is to discover why that should be. He is a man for whom an apparently insignificant detail may in truth well hold the greatest possible significance. Surely the mark of a truly great detective.'

'If you go on like this, I expect he'll arrest you.'

'When I do nothing but praise him?'

'Praise from you can be like the kiss of a shark.'

He laughed.

Alvarez reached the end of the dirt track from Ca Na Florina and turned on to the road which would take him through Biniarch. Scalfaro had been friendly and amusing and, despite his daughter's fears, never overstepping the point at which his light irony became objectionable rudeness. Because he had been able accurately to assess what would amuse and not anger a country inspector? Nicola had been sharp towards her father. Because there was often edge between them, or because he objected to her close friendship with Armitage?

CHAPTER 14

Alvarez passed the potted jungle and the raucous macaws in the foyer of the Hotel Trópico and spoke to one of the receptionists, who checked that Armitage was in his room. He took the lift up to the fourth floor.

Armitage, dressed only in shorts, spoke aggressively. 'You're in danger of making a goddamn nuisance of yourself. What the hell d'you mean by bothering Nicola?'

'I don't think I bothered her as much as her father . . . I was trying to discover why you have been lying to me.'

Armitage stared at him, bearded chin thrust forward. Then he muttered something that was incomprehensible, went over to the cupboard and opened the door with more force than was necessary. 'Brandy?'

'Thank you, señor. With—'

'With ice.' He carried a bottle of brandy and two glasses over to the small table, returned for the vacuum flask. 'How in the hell do I make you understand?'

'By telling me the truth.'

'You make it sound so bloody simple. But haven't you learned that my truth is different from yours and yours is different from the next man's?'

'Then tell me what yours is?'

Armitage poured out two drinks, added ice, passed one glass across to Alvarez, who had sat on the chair. He walked over to the window and looked out. 'What is my truth? Anything that will help me avoid confessing I acted like a shit.'

'In what way?'

'Give the alcohol time to circulate and dull my pride.' He turned and slumped down on the nearer bed. He drank, quickly and with little pleasure. As soon as the glass was empty, he got up and refilled it. 'Of course it was me who asked that woman where Sa Serra was,' he said as he returned to the bed.

'Just as it was you who attempted to break in?'

'I'm not talking myself into jail.'

'Then for the moment we will ignore the identity of the would-be burglar. Are you a friend of Señor Gaspari?'

'I've never met him.'

'Then why did you drive to Maranitx to discover where he lived?'

'I . . . Both Fermo and Nicola had talked about him.'

'How did you come to meet Señor Scalfaro?'

'I phoned and made an appointment.'

'And his daughter?'

'He introduced me to her.'

'Why did you phone him?'

'Because when I questioned Pedro, through the knuckleheaded waiter, there was a time when he became very excited and kept on mentioning two names. I asked the waiter what it was all about, but he was by then so contemptuous of Pedro that all he'd answer was that the old fool was totally crazy because he was going on and on about someone who disappeared and appeared . . . I didn't think it was all a load of nonsense. I reckoned Pedro was desperately trying to tell me something that he considered very important. I tried to get the waiter to treat Pedro seriously, but he wouldn't . . .

'The two names were Scalfaro and, as far as I could make out, Cabria. Back here, I checked through the telephone directory to find if either name appeared in it. Scalfaro did, once, Cabria didn't. I phoned Scalfaro and made an appointment to see him. I asked him if he'd ever known Pedro the Iceman or had visited Bassa Gris; he gave a definite no to both questions. I reckoned this probably proved the waiter had been right after all and Pedro had been talking nonsense, although there might just be another Scalfaro who wasn't on the telephone. I was getting ready to leave when Nicola returned home and he introduced me . . .'

'It was from the señora that you later learned about Señor Gaspari?'

After a while, Armitage nodded.

'And because of what you learned, you determined to find out more about him?'

'I . . .'

'Surely if a man is trying to discover the truth about his father's death, he is justified in pursuing any lead?'

'Is he?' Armitage's voice became harsh. 'When that lead's only offered because he's formed a special relationship with the person who's provided it? I used information which I obtained only because Nicola and I had become very fond of each other. A man who uses a woman's affections like that is a pure shit.'

'I do not agree.'

'Why not? Because it's part and parcel of your job all the time to use other people's confidences to their disadvantage?'

'Did you use the information to the señora's disadvantage?'

'No.'

'Then I cannot think that you should feel guilty.'

'You've a more accommodating conscience than I have.'

'What did the señora tell you that made you so curious about Señor Gaspari?'

'Does that matter?'

'Yes.'

'More than once, she said she couldn't understand the friendship between her father and Gaspari because Gaspari's a dour, rather stupid man and her father's full of life and very intelligent. And Gaspari once made some sort of pass at her and she complained to her father, who usually gets furious about that sort of thing, but even that didn't disturb the friendship. That made me wonder if Gaspari could have had any connection with the second man, Cabria, whom Pedro had mentioned.'

'And did he?'

Armitage shrugged his shoulders. 'Damned if I know. After I came up against that blank wall at the military base, I began to lose heart and having met Nicola . . . I'd discovered that that letter written by my father was almost certainly to my mother, he hadn't betrayed her, and she hadn't kept it from hate. If I couldn't discover exactly what had gone on, it didn't matter; nearly fifty years is a hell of a long time ago.'

'It still mattered sufficiently for you to try to break into Señor Gaspari's house—presumably to try and discover if he were in any way connected with Cabria.'

'I asked the woman where the house was. I didn't try to break into it.'

'I imagine you will not be surprised if I confess that I find it a little difficult to believe that? Señor, was it not your inability successfully to break into the house which finally decided you not to continue to try to uncover all the truth?'

'No.'

'I'm sorry.'

'That it wasn't me?'

'That I am still unable to believe your denial.'

'Prove I'm a liar.'

'I cannot.'

'Then all that's left for you to do is to relax and have another drink.'

Alvarez drove along the rising road that wound its way along the hills on the south-east side of Llueso Bay. The bay was at its most beautiful, all the development in the port sufficiently distant to be indistinct, and he thought that here man was as close to heaven as he was permitted to reach until he died and discovered where his resting-place was to be.

Two privates were on guard at the simple pole-barrier across the road and they watched him drive up and speak to them through the opened window with all the mindless disinterest of bored conscripts. 'Is Lieutenant Pons in the base?'

They shrugged their shoulders.

'Will you please find out?'

They resented his request but, accepting that someone who wished to talk to an officer might be of importance, one of them stepped into the small wooden hut to the side of the road and used the telephone inside. He called out: 'What's your name?'

'Inspector Alvarez of the Cuerpo General de Policía.'

The private disappeared from sight for a couple of minutes. When he reappeared, he pushed down on the counterweight so that the pole rose. 'The lieutenant'll be up at the barracks.'

Alvarez drove on. The road rose more steeply as it turned right to run between pine trees, then it forked. Since he could see buildings to the left, he chose to go that way.

A man in combat uniform, with lieutenant's rank, stood immediately outside the first of several wooden huts which stretched along the north side of a parade ground. Alvarez stopped the car. 'Lieutenant Pons?'

'That's right.'

He switched off the engine, put the car into gear since at that point there was a slight slope to the road, stepped out.

'Would you like to come in here?' Pons opened the door of the hut.

The room was sparsely furnished and those furnishings that there were possessed an institutional dinginess. Pons indicated the nearer, shabby chair. 'D'you like to sit?' As soon as Alvarez was seated, he said: 'Is something the matter?'

'Nothing that affects you directly, lieutenant.'

He looked relieved.

'I'm investigating the death of a man and in the course of my investigations have had reason to question Señor Armitage. Do you remember him?'

'Should I?'

'He's an Engishman who came here and tried to find out if his father had ever visited the base many years before.'

For a couple of seconds Pons's expression was blank, then he clicked his fingers. 'Of course! I'd forgotten his name.'

'He says you very kindly agreed to find out what you could, but the man you really wanted to talk to wasn't in the base that day.'

'That's right. Sargento Bauer has been around so long he knows everything—most especially, how close to insolence he can get without ending up on defaulters. I reckoned that if anyone could help the Englishman, he could.'

'You told Señor Armitage to come back the next day when you'd say if you'd been able to find out anything from this sargento—but when he did return, it seems an armed guard marched him in front of the colonel who threatened in broken English to have him shot.'

Pons laughed. 'The Old Man's a relic from the past. He reckons he's still entitled to kick any civilian up the backside and get away with it.'

'Had you mentioned the previous visit of the English señor to him?'

'No.'

'Then how did he know immediately what it was the Englishman wanted?'

'Presumably, through the grapevine. I'd had a word with another man; I expect he'd talked about a curious Englishman.'

'Did you speak to Sargento Bauer the day after you met Señor Armitage?'

'The next morning I was sent off to Oviedo before I had time to speak to anyone.'

'Presumably this was unexpected?'

'Very much so. My wife and I had been invited to a party she was really looking forward to and when I told her I was going to have to miss it, she gave me hell.'

'Was it an important mission in Oviedo.'

'As things turned out, it couldn't have been less so.'

'Then perhaps the real object of your going was to make certain you were not here when the Englishman returned?'

Pons looked at Alvarez, his face expressing first surprise, then uneasy curiosity. 'Who would have given a damn if I had spoken to him again?'

'The colonel, for one, judging from his talk of shooting spies.'

'He's a vintage blimp.'

'Possibly. But perhaps he'd had his orders and he carried them out with a little less subtlety than would have been wished?'

'Suppose you tell me just what in the hell this is all about?'

'I wish I knew.'

'You know enough to suggest I could have been shipped off to Oviedo to get me out of the way.'

'But I've no idea why that should be—and it is the why

which is so important. Did you ever have a word with the
sargento when you returned from Oviedo?'

'Yes, I did, in case the Englishman braved the colonel
and came back.'

'Was the sargento able to help?'

'He's not served as long as I've always thought and the
'forties were way before his time. All he could say was that
when he first came to the base, there was a vague rumour
of some Englishman who'd been buried here.'

'Could there be any truth in the story?'

'The army's taught me one thing—anything is possible,
provided only that it runs counter to common sense.'

'If an Englishman had been buried on the base, where
d'you think his grave would be?'

'In the cemetery—where else?'

'I'd like to go there and look for his grave.'

'First, tell me something. Do you really not know what
all this is about?'

'Almost fifty years ago something happened which involved an Englishman; it's possible there is a connection
between him and the base. Now, someone may be doing all
he can to make certain none of the facts comes to light.
That's all I can be certain about.'

'And you're trying to identify the something?'

'That's right.'

'I can't see that there's any harm in my helping you.'

They drove round the edge of the parade ground—
apparently to cross it in a car was a capital offence—and
along a road which skirted the edge of steep cliffs. This
brought them to the two-metre-high stone wall which en-
circled the cemetery. Alvarez climbed out of his car and
looked out at the bay and the sea beyond the headlands.
'This is a very beautiful place in which to be buried.'

'But not to live. The accommodation is some of the oldest
anywhere and the wives never stop complaining.'

They entered through a wide gateway, to the right of
which was a small chapel. It seemed that in spite of the

state of the accommodation, the base was a healthy place in which to live since most of the cemetery was down to grass and flowerbeds and only at the far end were there graves. Most of these were marked by simple headstones, but two had very elaborate ones in marble.

'Rank,' explained Pons, 'must be maintained at all times.'

They read the inscriptions on the headstones. All bore the names of Spaniards, together with their rank.

'It looks as if the vague rumour of the sargento's was no more than just that,' said Pons.

'Unless . . .' Alvarez was silent for a moment, then he said slowly, speaking to himself as much as to the other: 'The majority of the British are not Catholics and it is only recently that on this island it has been permitted for a non-Catholic to be buried within the walls of a cemetery. Perhaps his grave is outside.'

'In that case, you've one hell of a search ahead of you. There are hundreds of hectares of really rough land in the base.'

'But I don't think we need search all of them. The church is like the army, logically traditional.'

'I'll grant you the tradition, but not necessarily the logic. But what are you really saying?'

'That if a dead man can't, because of tradition, be placed within the cemetery, then the logical place in which to bury him is as close as possible. I would expect to find the grave, if there is one, close to the walls.'

It was half way along and a metre and a half out from the west wall. A wild rosemary bush had grown around and embraced it and branches of this had to be broken off before they could examine the crude concrete slab. Lichen had grown over this, but it rubbed off with little difficulty. The inscription, on three lines, was brief and potentially cryptic. PJA. 1942. RIP.

CHAPTER 15

Alvarez dialled the hotel and very soon was talking to Armitage. 'Good morning, señor.'

'What is it this time?'

He visualized the aggressive thrust of that bramblebush beard. 'I would like to know what were your father's initials?'

'Why?'

'To make certain of something.'

There was a pause. 'They were Perry James. What's the something?'

'I will explain when I see you tomorrow morning at your hotel.'

'And if I've arranged to be out all day?'

'I suggest you alter the arrangement.'

'Suggest or demand?'

'Will eleven o'clock suit you?'

'Look, if you're going to give orders, could you try to be less goddamn polite about giving them.'

After the call was over, Alvarez leaned back in the chair and stared at the top of the desk which was in its usual state of disorder. Perry James Armitage. PJA. 1942. RIP. Yet according to the official records, Perry Armitage had died in France. What did this mean?

The phone rang and Dolores answered it. She went through to the dining-room where Jaime and Alvarez were watching a football match. 'It's for you, Enrique.'

'Who is it?' he asked, without looking away from the screen.

'Señor Salas and he sounds to be in a temper.'

'Is he ever anything else?' Reluctantly, since Mallorca looked as if they might break with tradition and score a goal, he stood and made his way through to the other room.

It immediately became obvious that Salas was in a very bad temper indeed. 'Don't you ever do as you're damned well told?'

'I don't quite understand, señor.'

'That just about encapsulates your professional abilities. Did or did not Comisario Orifla inform you that investigations into the Gaspari case were concluded?'

'Yes, he did. But—'

'Does that or does that not mean that no further inquiries are to be carried out?'

'Yes, but—'

'Then why the devil have you disobeyed that order?'

'In what way have I done thât, señor?'

'You can ask? Damnit, I begin to wonder if you are in your right mind . . . Have you been making inquiries at Bassa Gris?'

'In a way, I suppose—'

'Were those inquiries connected with the Gaspari case?'

'That is just possible—'

'You are to cease immediately all further inquiries into the case or into any matter which is, or may be, connected, however remotely, with it. Have I put that into sufficiently simple terms for you to comprehend?'

'I understand what you're saying, señor, but not why you are saying it.'

'We may be having to live in a period of socialized democracy but, thank God, that still does not mean that an inspector has the right to question the orders of his superiors.'

'I wasn't exactly doing that—'

'Do you ever know what you're doing, even inexactly? Should you continue to pursue these investigations, in whatever form, you will be guilty of disobeying orders. Do you know the consequences of that?'

'Yes, señor.'

The connection was cut.

Alvarez replaced the receiver, lit a cigarette. His visit to

the base had alerted someone to the fact that he was still
trying to uncover the truth and that someone had the power
to demand that Salas threaten him with dismissal from the
force if he continued to disobey orders. There could be no
question of his ignoring the order this time. Incompetence
was accepted, since it was a tradition, but flagrant dis-
obedience of a direct order was not. Let him continue, and
be seen to be continuing, the investigation and then he
would be sacked, with loss of all pension rights. He had
become too old willingly to accept that as the price which
must be paid if truth were to be illuminated. Did he even
dare tell Armitage about the grave? The answer was obvious.
Tomorrow's appointment must be cancelled—luckily, he
had given no hint why he'd requested it. If Armitage
learned his father's grave was on the base, he would demand
to visit it. Such a visit would make it obvious that Inspector
Alvarez had continued to disobey his superior chief . . .

He returned to the dining-room just in time to see Mallorca's goalkeeper fumble the ball and concede a goal. He
crossed to the sideboard and, ignoring Dolores's evident
disapproval, brought out a bottle of brandy.

The telephone call came through at 10.15 the next morning,
five minutes after he'd arrived in the office, a trifle late
through oversleeping.

A man, very breathless, said: 'Is that the inspector? For
God's sake come quickly. My house has been burgled and
I've lost everything. The safe's been emptied and all the
paintings have gone.'

'What's your name and address?'

'Chamorro. I live at Ca'n Taro, Estalpa. If the thieves
get the paintings off the island . . . One of them's worth
millions and it's not properly insured . . .'

Alvarez cut short the other's lamentations, said he'd be
along as soon as possible, rang off. The caller had been
speaking Castilian, which almost certainly meant he was
from the Peninsula. That a valuable painting had not been

fully insured suggested he had not dared to insure it for its full value because he had not made an honest declaration of his wealth to tax officials. A smart businessman from Madrid who'd been making a fortune, but declaring only a modest income and investing the tax thus saved in possessions which could be easily concealed?

He went down to the street and along to where he had parked his car. He cut through the village to the Laraix road, which took him through the valley—Cousin Francisca's land was out of sight to his left—and up into the mountains that were in parts lunar-like in their bleakness.

The road skirted Laraix monastery, in which rested a sacred relic to which the faithful had prayed for centuries, and then once more passed through land in which there was only an occasional building, usually in ruins, to mark where men and women had once struggled to wrest a subsistence living from bitter ground.

Twenty minutes after passing Laraix, he reached Estalpa, a small village which owed its existence and its survival to the narrow valley in which it lay; a valley of plenty in the middle of mountainous desolation. An old man directed him to take the left-hand fork beyond the village and the road soon left the valley and began to climb in a series of hairpins, each one seemingly more acute than the last.

He reached an outcrop of rock to come in sight of a house; on the right-hand gatepost at the beginning of the drive was a nameboard—Ca'n Taro. Set on a rock shelf a hundred metres above the road, the large, modern house had a magnificent view of the valley and the mountains which enclosed it. A house which had cost twice as much to build as it would have done on a more accessible site.

The drive was steep and unfenced and as he climbed it at a snail's pace he tried not to look at the drop, cursing himself for such cowardice. The garage was two metres below the level of the house and in front of it there was just enough room for a sharp three-point turn. As he made this, his mind filled with pictures of failing brakes . . . He applied the handbrake, switched off the engine, left the gear in reverse. He was sweating as hard as if he had run up from the road instead of having driven.

He climbed the broad steps up to the house, almost stifled by the heat that was even greater because of the rock face. All the shutters were closed, but he did not immediately place any significance in the fact since it was the custom—though not always among foreigners—to keep the sun out of the interior. But when he tried the door and found that locked and he rang the bell and there was no answer, he accepted that there was no one in. He swore. How typical to call for help and then rush off . . .

There was a clatter of stone and he turned. A man had appeared around the corner of the house. 'Señor Chamorro?' he called out as he took a pace forward. His right shoe landed on a small chip of rock and skidded and he had to move very quickly to keep his balance; as he moved, there was an explosion which echoed against the rock and he suffered a stinging pain along the outside of his left arm.

He would never have described himself as a man of quick reactions, yet he was sprinting for the corner of the house before his mind consciously accepted that he'd been shot at.

There was a second shot. On the rock face directly ahead of him, which backed the house, there appeared a starred scar where the bullet struck and shattered. As he ran, he weaved from side to side. There was a third shot and he heard the wicked screech of a ricocheting bullet.

His issue automatic was back at the post where he always kept it because guns frightened him. So his only hope of escape lay in flight. He reached the corner of the house and the cover this offered. Instinct told him to keep running; reason said to slow long enough to assess the situation. Reason won. The gunman would not know he was unarmed and would probably assume that, having reached cover, he would draw his own gun and return the fire. Then it would not be wise to crowd him. Against that, time was limited for the gunman because he might just be able to attract the attention of a passing motorist—though traffic was very light—or he might even have a transceiver on which he could summon help, provided the mountains were not making radio communication impossible . . . If he were the gunman, what would he do? Continue direct pursuit— which might lead to his being ambushed—or retire and perhaps take up position by the Ibiza as he decided the best way of nailing his quarry?

There were only four windows and one doorway at the rear of the house, hardly surprising since the almost sheer rock face was only three metres away. The two ground-floor windows were shuttered, the door was locked. But was the door also bolted? Not if the last person out had left by that and not the front door.

Life as a detective had taught him several arcane skills and in his left-hand trouser pocket he always carried 'something which might come in useful'—a steel cylinder, confiscated from a very able burglar, which contained small, beautifully made skeleton keys which resembled dentist's probes.

He opened the cylinder and slid the four keys into the palm of his left hand, chose one and inserted this into the lock. As he worked, searching through feel for the very slight 'give' which would tell him this key might force the lock, he tried to act upon something the burglar had ruefully said to him—more haste, less heed (he'd been so busy at his work, he'd not heard Alvarez approach). Yet how to work coolly when an armed man could come into view at any second . . .

From his right came a sound. He whirled round, sickly certain that he would face a drawn gun. There was nothing. A small sliver of rock must have fallen from somewhere above. Breathing very quickly, sweating profusely, sick in the stomach, wishing he were a man able to face danger with at least a semblance of fortitude, he withdrew the key and inserted a second one. As he manœuvred this, he strained his ears for the slight sound that this time would not be a falling chip but the gunman, finally catching up . . . The tumblers turned at a moment when his fear had become so keen that he was not conscious of what he was doing.

The door was not bolted. He stepped inside, bolted it, and felt the weakness of relief; a relief that was very temporary because his safety could be only temporarily certain. He was in the kitchen. He went from there into the entrance hall, gloomy because of the closed shutters, but not so gloomy that he could not see the telephone on a small table. There had been no exterior lines—it would cost two fortunes to connect by line a house as isolated as this—and so it must work by radio. There was dust everywhere, suggesting the house had not been lived in for weeks, so would the phone still be operating? By its side was a small card on which were the instructions. He lifted the receiver and pressed down the green button. There was no high-pitched, ululating sound which would have meant he could press down the yellow button and dial. The phone was not operating.

There was the sound of breaking wood. One of the shutters at the front was being smashed. The gunman had satisfied himself his quarry, probably unarmed after all, must have withdrawn into the houe; he was now intent on cornering and murdering him.

Alvarez knew a childish urge to run, wildly and with no more reason than to get as far as possible from the point of danger, but still could summon up the self-control to recognize that to do so would be to sign his own death warrant. Did he hide? If he could find somewhere, then so could the gunman . . . He realized he had only one chance and this called for his playing on the gunman's fears while managing to overcome his own. He shouted: 'The line's terrible because it's radio. I said, Ca'n Taro . . . If you know the place, then get here bloody fast. He must have left his car some way away, so you'll be able to corner him if you block the road in both directions . . . Yeah, I'm armed.'

He waited, motionless, tension constricting his breathing.

One fact was in his favour: almost every criminal, when actually committing a crime, was nervous enough to believe the worst. The gunman might not stop to wonder if a radio telephone would have been left operational in an empty house . . .

The only sounds were the distant shrilling of countless cicadas; no slap of shoes on the tiled floor, no rustle of clothes. Alvarez counted up to sixty; another sixty; a third sixty. And as there was still no sound of his pursuer, he began to dare to believe that his bluff had worked.

CHAPTER 16

Dr Rossello, self-satisfied and pompous, was seldom as sympathetic as his patients would have wished. 'It's no more than a scratch,' he said, as he finished examining the ten-centimetre score along Alvarez's forearm.

'It stings like hell.'

'Quite possibly. I'll dust it with antibiotic powder and stick on a plaster; do the same again before you go to bed tonight and first thing in the morning. If it doesn't clear up within four days, come back.'

Alvarez left the surgery and walked along the pavement which, being on the east side of the street, was still in shade. He looked up at the mountains which backed Llueso; he watched a couple, arms around one another, oblivious to the rest of the world; he saw a woman leave the bakery and noted the two barras in her shopping basket and he imagined the mouth-watering scent of their crusts; a Mobylette came down the road and on the back was strapped a wooden box in which sat a what-hound, muzzle pointing into wind; he listened to two men have a brief, furious row which ended as abruptly as it had begun and in raucous laughter . . . Ordinary, everyday events which for him gained an extraordinary significance because he had so nearly died.

He took the first turning to the left and went into the bar/ restaurant half way along where he had two brandies. Never before had brandy tasted so good.

Back home, Isabel and Juan were watching the television and could not be bothered to greet him as they should have done. He smiled with amused understanding. Dolores was in the kitchen and when he entered she was standing at the stove so that her back was to him. 'Whatever it is you're cooking,' he said enthusiastically, 'it smells absolutely delicious.'

She turned, saw the plaster on his arm immediately below the short sleeve of his shirt. 'Enrique, what's happened?' she asked with immediate, sharp concern. 'What have you done to your arm?'

'It's only a scratch,' he replied with dismissive bravery, echoing words which earlier he had so resented.

'But how did you get it?'

'A man took a shot at me, but didn't aim quite straight.'

'Mother of God!' She began to tremble. She was a woman of strong emotions, of which the strongest was love of her family. When any of them was threatened, she tended to panic.

He suffered a sense of guilt, knowing that he had given the news baldly in order to present himself as a man who scorned danger. 'It's all over and done with and all I have is this small graze.'

'But if you'd been killed . . .' She reached out and pulled him to her, needing the physical reassurance that he was still alive. 'He could have killed you.'

'But he didn't. So have a drink to celebrate?'

She didn't say no. He disengaged himself and went through to the dining-room where he poured out two large brandies. Back in the kitchen, Dolores was still standing where he had left her and she watched him intently as if frightened that should she look away even for a second, he might vanish. He opened the refrigerator, brought out an ice tray, and put three cubes in each glass. As he picked up one glass to hand to her, Jaime entered.

'That,' said Jaime enthusiastically, 'is what I call service!'

'It's for Dolores,' replied Alvarez as he passed it to her.

Jaime stared at his wife in astonishment. 'You're boozing at this time?'

'Don't be more of a fool than you have to be,' she snapped, grateful for the chance to ease some of her emotional tension. 'Don't you realize, he could be dead?'

'Who can't?'

'Sometimes I think you are already. Take him out of here, Enrique, before I lose my temper. It's not fitting for a wife to say exactly what she thinks of her husband in front of someone else.'

Jaime looked at her, then at Alvarez. 'But I don't understand . . .'

Alvarez pushed him towards the doorway into the dining-room. 'The bottle's on the table.'

As they left the kitchen, she wondered how she could best honour the miracle of Alvarez's escape? Was there still time to go out and buy some gambas? She decided there was.

Dolores returned to the dining-room, which she had left ten minutes earlier, settled in her chair and used the remote control to switch off the sound on the television because the advertisements were beginning. She said to Alvarez: 'I've just had a word with Cousin Francisca and she says she's very glad indeed that you escaped being seriously wounded. She hopes you'll very soon be better.'

'You shouldn't have bothered to tell her.'

'Not tell her, when you were so nearly killed? She would never have forgiven me.'

'Worried about him, is she?' asked Jaime.

'Naturally, since he's family.'

'That's not exactly what I meant . . .'

'Just keep your meanings to yourself so that we don't have to suffer any more of your stupidity . . . Enrique, she says that just as soon as you feel fit enough, she'd like to see you.' The advertisements came to an end and she pressed the button to re-activate the sound.

Alvarez's mind wandered. Next to Cousin Francisca's finca was a field and he'd recently heard that the owner had become too old to work it and wanted to sell. It would be very interesting to have this extra land and, braving the scorn of the more reactionary neighbours, try growing on it some of the unusual fruits and vegetables which were now reaching the island—avocado pears, limes, kiwis . . .

Dolores hurried out of the kitchen to answer the phone, hurried back and said to Alvarez: 'It's the post.'

He looked up at the electric clock on the wall. 'What's got them shouting so early in the morning?' He dunked another piece of coca in the hot chocolate and ate this as he made his way to the phone.

The cabo told him that Comisario Orifla had arrived at the station and was creating hell because there was no sign of the lazy bastard of an inspector. Alvarez replied that he'd be along as soon as possible and in the meantime to tell the commisario that Inspector Alvarez had rung through from the port to say that he'd been unexpectedly called down there, but would return as soon as he could. Back in the kitchen, he resumed his breakfast.

Initially, it was difficult to make out the reason for Orifla's visit. He had the aggressive, chip-on-the-shoulder attitude common to small men and the more he tried to rein in his natural manner, the more a slight speech impediment was magnified so that many of his words became mangled. All the time he was attempting to express his, and Superior Chief Salas's, relief at Alvarez's escape in terms which were far stronger than came naturally to him, many of his words were incomprehensible. But when that duty was over, his speech once more became clipped and lucid. He said that the owner of Ca'n Taro, a well-known and very respectable businessman, had been in Bilbao for the past three months and knew nothing about what had happened. So the only

lead the police had at the moment was Alvarez's description
of the gunman. 'And that is, to say the least, extremely
vague. I would have expected you to be able to provide a
far more detailed one.'

Alvarez decided that it would be a waste of time to try to
explain that when one suddenly found oneself looking down
the barrel of a gun, one did not—unless brave—have much
room in one's mind for recording the features of the man
who held it.

There was a long pause.

'Inspector, do you smoke?' Orifla asked and already the
edges of some of his words had begun to blur.

'As a matter of fact, I do, señor.'

Orifla brought out a silver cigarette case from his coat
pocket and proffered it. He snapped open a lighter. Alvarez,
slightly bewildered by this continuing display of good manners, leaned forward to light the cigarette.

'Inspector, what cases are you investigating in which
someone under suspicion might be desperate enough to
attempt to kill you?'

'Only one, señor, and that's the Gaspari/Segui case.'

'How can you be so certain?'

'After this, the only serious crime I'm investigating is a
robbery in one of the urbanizacíons down in the port. The
probable thief would never turn to violence.'

'The would-be assassin may not be connected with a case
presently under investigation, but with one from the recent
past.'

'I've checked all my work for the past six months.'

'You're very definite.'

'Yes, I am, señor.'

'You're convinced that this attempt to murder you was a
direct result of your inquiries into the attempted burglary
of Señor Gaspari's house and the death of Segui?'

'Yes, I am.'

'Do I have to remind you that there is still no proof
that Segui did not fall accidentally? Again, no connection

whatsoever between his death and the attempted burglary has been established.'

'Señor Armitage is connected with both of them.'

'I would hardly call that a decisive link; certainly far from sufficient to lead to the assumption you're trying to make.'

'There is a much stronger one.'

'What is that?'

'In both cases, pressure is being exerted to prevent an investigation proceeding and succeeding.'

'That is a reckless claim.'

'You told me that the Gaspari case was closed even before I had submitted my report. Somebody gave the order to vanish the hairs taken from under Segui's nail. Why is someone so desperate to hide the fact that, although Señor Armitage's father is supposed to have died in France, his grave is in Bassa Gris?'

'It's what?'

'His grave, señor, is immediately outside the cemetery that is within the base.'

Orifla could not conceal his shocked perturbation.

'In England there has obviously been a cover-up for nearly fifty years; and here it has to be the same. Only the highest authority in each country could have ordered such a thing. What happened all those years ago that must not even now be revealed? What did Pedro the Simple know that made him so dangerous he had to be murdered? Why was a British naval officer on this island in the middle of the Second World War and why was he buried in such secrecy? Who is still so desperate to keep the truth hidden?'

Orifla stubbed out his cigarette. He said, speaking slowly, but distinctly: 'It would seem, Inspector, that you are a man of greater perspicacity than is at first apparent . . . a perspicacious man accepts that there are times when, because he cannot see the whole picture, he inevitably gains a distorted view of that small part which is visible. Do you follow me?'

'I'm not quite certain.'

'I am saying that because he has a necessarily distorted viewpoint, he may well be unable correctly to appreciate what course of action he should take. In such circumstances, it is clearly right for him to take none.'

'Are you suggesting, señor, that I should forget all the questions I have just asked? But if I do not find out the answers, there may well be a second attempt to murder me.'

Orifla lit another cigarette. 'The superior chief appreciates that your life may well continue to be at risk and, ever mindful of the welfare of those who serve under him, he therefore suggests that you take leave of absence on full pay. The Guardía, as you will know, have a holiday camp on the coast near Malaga where officers and men can take their families at small cost to themselves. He will arrange for you and your family to occupy one of the officers' houses for an extended period, thereby ensuring your safety.'

It was a very tempting offer. It would remove him from danger. His silence would please his superiors and a humble inspector was a fool if he did not seize the chance to do that. But he came from peasant stock and throughout most of history peasants had possessed little of value beyond their own self-respect and therefore they had defended this with all their natural cunning and tenacity, using any twisted and tortuous means available when direct opposition to authority could mean their own destruction. 'Señor, if I am right in my suppositions, then perhaps I would not be safe even if I were off the island; those who wish me dead might well pursue me wherever I go. I believe that my safety can only be secured by naming those who tried to arrange my murder and therefore, unless the superior chief orders me not to, I intend to continue my investigations.'

Orifla stared at him with a growing anger. 'Don't you understand that his sole reason for making this offer is his concern for your safety?'

Salas's sole concern, thought Alvarez, was to try to secure his own safety at a time when he found himself in a near-

impossible situation. He'd ordered a cessation of the investigations into the break-in at Gaspari's house because
pressure had been put on him to do so; he had known that
he always could, on reasonable grounds, be able to justify
his actions in a case that was apparently of such little
consequence. But now there had been an attempted murder
of one of his inspectors and neither he, if called upon to do
so, nor those above him, could ever hope to justify the
closing down of this investigation. Therefore, even though
he continued to be pressed to find a way of having it closed
down, the only way open to him of doing this in safety was
to bribe his inspector into agreeing not to pursue it. 'It is
very kind of the superior chief to be so concerned, señor,
but I am convinced that the only way to ensure my safety
in the long term is to pursue my investigations.'

'Naturally, I cannot order you to change your mind.'
Orifla was furious. He had come to Llueso expecting to
meet a country inspector who would easily be persuaded to
get everyone off the hook, and not only had he failed but he
couldn't understand why, when he was so much cleverer.

After Orifla had left, Alvarez reached down to the bottom
right-hand drawer of the desk and brought out of it a bottle
and glass. He poured himself a very generous brandy. He
was frightened. Originally, Salas had ordered him to cease
his inquiries into the Gaspari burglary and he had had to
obey. So those who had forced Salas to make the order could
have had no reason to plan his murder. Then someone else
needed to silence him. When he had said that he preferred
to remain in Llueso in order to work to unmask the would-be
murderer because this might well be the only way in which
to ensue his own safety, those had been words of plain,
unvarnished truth.

He drained the glass, refilled it.

CHAPTER 17

When a man believes he must again become the target for murder unless he can quickly uncover the truth, any delay in the investigations becomes very frightening. Throughout Sunday, when all he could do was wait and drink, Alvarez suffered a growing tension which became so great that it took him quite some time to fall asleep after lunch. On Monday, he astonished Dolores by arriving downstairs for breakfast at ten to eight.

As soon as he reached his office he telephoned Palma and asked a clerk in the Ministry of the Interior to find out as much as she could about the residencias issued to Giovanni Gaspari and Fermo Scalfaro. He said she might have to check back a little while.

She rang back on Tuesday morning and complained bitterly and at length at the task he'd given her. Finally, she said: 'The residencias were first issued in nineteen forty-four. They were permanent so they have never needed renewing, which is why it was so difficult to trace them.'

'I've never before heard of a permanent residencia.'

'No more have I. And there's something else that's odd about them. I'll bet you can't guess why they were issued?'

'Because the Governor-General ordered they should be?'

'You knew?' She sounded disappointed.

'I guessed when you made it obvious that there was something unusual about the issuing.'

'Then you can guess something else that's unusual?'

'Not this time.'

'Among the accompanying papers there's a handwritten note to the effect that their names were formerly Filippo Nicolazzi and Count Alfred Capria.'

He whistled. 'That really is news! . . . Will you spell out those names so I get them exactly right?'

She did so.

He told her she'd performed wonders, thanked her profusely, rang off. He stared down at the sheet of paper on which he'd written the names. Something about them seemed familiar, yet he couldn't place what . . . He forgot that puzzle and concentrated on larger ones. Two Italians had been granted special, possibly unique, residencias in the middle of a world war; one of them (and maybe both) had been granted a licence to own a handgun; both those grants had been made on the order of the Governor-General who, in normal circumstances, would never have concerned himself with such minor administrative matters. Ergo, these matters weren't minor, but very major. How? Why? What thread connected them with the dead Perry J. Armitage, buried at Bassa Gris; connected them nearly fifty years later with the death of a simple Mallorquin and all the events which had followed that?

As sometimes happened when one forgot one problem to concentrate on another, one's mind returned to, and solved, the first. When, with the help of the waiter, Armitage had been questioning Pedro, Pedro had become very excited and had mentioned two names—Scalfaro and Cabria. Cabria and Capria were so similar that Alvarez was certain the former was a mispronunciation of the latter. Then Pedro had been saying that he'd known the two when Gaspari had still been using his original name . . .

The phone rang and he lifted the receiver. Gaspari had been found dead.

Very occasionally, meteorological conditions during summer were such that in parts of the mountains clouds formed while the rest of the island remained bathed in brilliant sunshine; this condition was known as shepherds' weather, not because the shade brought relief to the flocks, but because the clouds resembled a fleece (that was, provided one had a good imagination). Shepherds' weather had brought a gloom to the valley which was in keeping with sudden death.

Alvarez stared at the body which lay on the concrete path which surrounded the house, then up at the small balcony with wrought-iron railings.

'You're probably thinking,' said the doctor, 'that since he was a foreigner, he fell over the edge after having too much to drink.'

'I don't know that I was thinking anything definite,' said Alvarez.

'It's the obvious conclusion.'

'But there's a reason why I shouldn't accept that?'

'There certainly is.'

The doctor, decided Alvarez, was one of those who believed that his professional qualifications and position raised him high. Nevertheless, experience suggested that in order to gain full cooperation it would be best if he appeared to accept such an assessment. 'You've found out something already?' he asked, his tone full of respect.

'Look here.'

He leaned over visually to examine the dead man's head, an unwelcome task since Gaspari had landed on it.

'D'you see that?' 'That' was a sliver of wood. 'There's no wood down here, so he couldn't have collected that from the fall.'

He had been certain it was murder before he had arrived—not that he was going to let the doctor know that—and this all but confirmed the fact. He imagined the scene. Gaspari, his wits possibly dulled by drink, had been lured out on to the balcony. The murderer, a length of wood in his hand, had delivered a blow fierce enough to rip off the sliver of wood. Either Gaspari had slumped over the rails and fallen, or the murderer had lifted him up and over and let him drop so that he landed on his head, sustaining injuries that were designed to hide those already inflicted. 'What sort of weapon am I looking for?'

'A length of fairly stout soft wood, to judge from the look

of the sliver. Of course, you'll get an expert to confirm that.' His tone said that this would be pure formality. 'You'll arrange for the body to be removed to the mortuary and for the PM?'

'Yes . . . But just before you go, will you give an estimate of the time of death?'

'Ten hours ago.'

'I imagine that that isn't any more precise than usual?'

The doctor, who did not like any of his utterances to be treated so cavalierly, nodded curtly, bade Alvarez the briefest of goodbyes, crossed to his new Sierra and drove off.

Alvarez turned and walked round the house to the front door. He stepped inside and called out. As he waited, he stared at an oil painting of a large house in rolling countryside; he wondered whether this existed or whether it was mainly the product of an artist's imagination . . . His vague thoughts were interrupted by the sounds of shoes slapping on tiles and Elena came into the entrance hall. He said he'd like to ask her a few questions and suggested they went through to the sitting-room. Once in there, she stood with arms folded across her chest.

'This may take a little time, so why not sit?'

She settled with awkward, ungainly movements. 'Señorita, will you tell me what happened, especially about anything unusual?'

She had a hoarse voice, as if incubating a bad cold, and spoke almost without any change of tone. She had left her home in the village at 8.30 in the morning and had ridden in on her Mobylette. Because the señor had died on the south side of the house, she had not immediately noticed the body. The back door, as was usual, had been shut and locked. She had gone through to the kitchen and put on her apron. The Inspector wanted to know about anything unusual. On the draining-board there had been a dirty glass.

'What's odd about that?' he asked, perplexed.

'The señor was a very lazy man,' she replied, ignoring the

Mallorquin custom which dictated that any newly deceased, even if a foreigner, was bereft of vice. 'He could never be bothered to carry anything through to the kitchen, except the butter and cheese which he put in the fridge, so I'd find dirty glasses in the sitting-room and all the remains of supper in the dining-room. Didn't matter what dirty things get like in this heat. Have you ever heard of such laziness?'

He said he hadn't. What had she done next?'

She had walked into the dining-room and cleared up the remains of supper; he had not finished the lettuce and what was left in the bowl had had to be thrown away. He had never learned that a peseta wasted was two pesetas spent. The dining-room cleared, she had checked the downstairs sitting-room; since he seldom used it, there had been nothing dirty lying around. She'd pulled back the curtains and opened the windows and then the shutters and that was when she'd first seen the body. She had immediately tele-phoned the guardía and that was all she knew.

He complimented her on her memory and thanked her for being so careful; she seemed to be indifferent both to his praise and his gratitude. He suggested that now he'd spoken to her, much the best idea for her was to return home.

He went upstairs. The stairs led directly into the sala, a large space once used to dry animal food, such as algarroba beans, off which led three bedrooms and a bathroom. Gaspari had turned the sala into an upstairs sitting-room. In one corner was a large television set, with video and satellite receiver underneath it, and a stacked music centre by its side. Against a wall were three long shelves, the top two of which were filled with video cassettes and the bottom one with compact discs and long-playing records. It became clear that Gaspari's tastes had not been of the most refined; the music was pop and a number of the videos were porno-graphic.

He crossed the floor—carpeted only in the middle—to the French windows, which were open, and went out on to the balcony. There was a scratch on the top rail, otherwise there was nothing which might mark the death. He returned inside and went over to a small table against the far wall. On this was a bottle of Larios gin, a three-parts-empty bottle of tonic, and a glass. He sniffed the glass; it seemed to have the faint aroma of whisky.

He turned and stared out at the balcony and imagined himself to be the murderer, determined to kill and to hide his murder under the guise of an accident. He'd encourage Gaspari to drink—almost certainly, not a difficult task. He'd use a wooden weapon because wood could be burned. He'd lure Gaspari out on to the balcony on some pretext, smash the wood down on his skull, and if he didn't topple over, tip him up to land head first down on the concrete, suffering further injuries that would hide the initial ones . . .

So there were several things to search for—signs of blood near, or on, the balcony; a length of wood, or the ashes of same; a glass which had contained gin and tonic; and any foreign object which would suggest the presence of a second man—though what in this context was foreign it was impossible to say beforehand.

There was a wood-burning stove at the far end of the room. He opened the doors and found a pile of ash inside. Assuming that the stove had been cleared by Elena at the end of winter—an assumption that would be checked—then here was evidence, though not proof, of the burning of the weapon.

He went downstairs to his car for the powerful torch he always carried in it. Because the sunlight was so brilliant, the interior of the sala was, by contrast, dim. He knelt on the tiled floor clear of the carpet, and shone the beam of the torch across the tiles in front of the French windows at an angle which he altered after each sweep. About to give up, a tiny patch of what appeared to be glossy varnish suddenly appeared. Under artificial light and against a dark background, blood often looked like that. Tests would have to be made to determine whether this was human blood and if so, and if possible, to identify its group and compare that with Gaspari's; perhaps even, with the miracle of DNA testing, specifically to name it Gaspari's.

It was popular wisdom that there could be no meeting between people, between people and things, or between things, which did not leave traces. The difficulty was in finding them and, having found them, in identifying them for what they were. He got down on hands and knees and began to search the floor. Eleven minutes after starting he found an empty cover of book matches which had been thrown into the waste-paper basket. Printed on the front was the name Hotel Trópico.

He went downstairs and through to the kitchen. Luck was with him. Elena had stacked all the dirty plates and crockery from the dining-room on the draining-board, but one glass stood apart and he optimistically assumed that this was the one she had seen there on her arrival and which had so surprised her. Had she not told him how the señor was too lazy ever to clear the table, he wouldn't have thought twice about that one glass, but it was of an unusual and elegant shape and it matched the one on the table upstairs, which had seemed to smell of whisky, not gin. If Gaspari had known his murderer—and surely he must have done to have let him into the house?—what more natural than that he should offer drinks and they should both enjoy these in the upstairs sitting-room, perhaps watching the television? And after the murder, wishing to conceal the fact of his presence, the murderer had taken his glass, removed the bottle of whisky, and put the glass down on the draining-board where, normally, it could be expected to go unremarked. But however self-possessed a man might think himself to be, after committing a murder he suffered panic. The murderer had mistaken the glasses . . . All supposition, but a test for prints might quickly prove whether or not the supposition were correct.

CHAPTER 18

Maranitx was a small village, yet even so there were three banks which faced each other across the square. The manager of the third, a small man who wore horn-rimmed spectacles that kept slipping down his nose, said: 'Señor Gaspari is a customer of ours, yes.'

'I'm afraid he died last night,' said Alvarez.

'Very sad. But of course he was not a young man. It must have been sudden because I saw him the other day and he looked quite fit.'

'He fell and fractured his skull.'

The manager picked up a pencil and fiddled with it. 'The Cuerpo General de Policía are not usually interested in accidents.' He looked up, his dark brown eyes sharp. The spectacles slid slowly down his nose, but not until they reached as far as they could go did he push them back into place.

'Right now, I'm trying to establish whether or not it was an accident . . . It would help if I knew something about his financial affairs. I could, of course, go through the usual channels to apply for an examination order, but that always takes time.'

'What doesn't?' The manager's brief smile temporarily banished his look of pernicketiness.

'So I'm wondering if you can give me general details of his account?'

'Without an order, general details perhaps, specific ones no.'

'Fair enough. What I'd like to know is how well off he was, where his income came from, whether he had investments . . . All that sort of thing.'

'I'll check with our records and then pass on as much as seems proper.'

There was a fifteen-minute wait, during which Alvarez leafed through a copy of *Ultima Hora*, before the manager said: 'I'm afraid that what I can tell you probably won't help very much. Señor Gaspari has banked with us for many years, but the only services he's ever called on were those connected with a current account. At the beginning of each week he paid in a cheque drawn on a bank in Liechtenstein; the money was withdrawn during the week. As far as our knowledge goes, he owned no investments.'

'A Liechtenstein bank and not an Italian one? . . . If you judge by the size of the weekly cheque, was he a rich man?'

'Rich is a word, Inspector, that at any one time means different things to different people. You'll remember as clearly as I the days when a thousand-peseta note was rarely seen because it represented so much spending power. Now, they are to be replaced by coins because their value has dropped so low . . . But to return to your question. By my standards, he was rich indeed. If I had available the amount he withdrew each week, my lifestyle would be luxurious.'

'Can you give me the name of the bank in Liechtenstein?'

'Only when you present me with an order authorizing me to do so. However—' again that brief smile—'I don't imagine you would find the results worth the effort. If you asked the bank in question to give you full details of the señor's account, you would be given a very dusty answer. Since modern taxation has been introduced into this country, any number of Spaniards have discovered to their satisfaction that the Liechtenstein banks are very secretive.'

'Then I imagine that there's not much more you can tell me?'

'Nothing more.'

Alvarez thanked the other, said goodbye, left. He began to cross the square in the direction of his parked car, changed his mind and went over to the nearest table set in front of a café and in the shade of an acacia. After a while, a yawning waiter took his order of a coffee cortado and a brandy.

He lit a cigarette. In terms of income, Gaspari had been

a rich, perhaps a very rich, man. In the course of each week
he had drawn a very considerable sum of money. Yet Sa
Serra could not have cost very much to run, even allowing
for Elena's wages, and since he'd been described as a recluse,
he clearly hadn't led a very full social life. So on what or on
whom had he spent all that money?

Alvarez checked at the reception desk of the Hotel Trópico
that Armitage was in his room, took the lift up to the fourth
floor.

Armitage's greeting was typically robust. 'Can't I damn
well go even a couple of days without your phoning
and demanding a meeting? What the bloody hell is it this
time?'

'I need to ask you a few questions about Monday night.'

Armitage crossed to the table on which he'd set out a
bottle, two glasses, and the vacuum flask. 'While I pour, sit
down and explain what's so goddamn important about
Monday night that you have to drag me off the beach?'

'Señor Scalfaro has not told you?'

'Not told me what?' Armitage poured out two brandies.

'That Señor Gaspari died on Monday night.'

Armitage swung round to stare at Alvarez. 'Well I'm
damned! . . . No, Fermo hadn't told me, but then I haven't
seen him for a few days.' He unscrewed the lid of the vacuum
flask and brought out ice cubes, which he dropped into the
glasses. 'It must have been pretty sudden. What was the
cause—heart?'

'He fell from the balcony of the upstairs sitting-room.'

'The poor old sod! Still, he can't have known much about
it and that's a kinder death than most of us are allowed.'
He handed a glass to Alvarez.

'You do not seem distressed by the news!'

'It's hypocritical to be distressed over the death of someone one doesn't know. I'm guilty of many faults, but hypo-
crisy isn't one of them.'

'It is possible that his death was not accidental.'

'You're saying he may have been murdered?' Armitage sat on the nearer bed.

'It is possible, yes.'

'You're a man for whom everything seems to be bloody possible. Suppose you come down off the fence for once. Was he or wasn't he murdered?'

'I cannot answer because I don't yet know.'

'And you're here because you think I may be able to help?'

'That is so.'

'Then you're out of bloody luck. Never met the man.'

'He was a friend of Señor Scalfaro and you are often at the señor's house.'

'And?'

'Have you never seen Señor Gaspari there?'

'No.'

'Will you tell me something, señor? Where were you on Monday night?'

'Here.'

'You did not see the señora?'

'She's had to visit relatives who live near Barcelona because one of 'em's ill and Spaniards are very quick to prepare themselves for heaven.'

'Did you leave the hotel that evening?'

'I went out for a meal.'

'Why, when the hotel has a restaurant?'

'Their food is aimed at the Bromley housewife who feels she's risking being poisoned if she's offered anything she can't buy in her home town.'

'Where did you eat?'

'In a bar/restaurant a couple of kilometres along the coast. You'd never find anyone from Bromley there. No tablecloths, the menu's written on a blackboard, the waiter looks as if he's suffering from something nasty, and the food's delicious.'

'Did you return here immediately after the meal?'

'I drove around the countryside for a while.'

'For how long?'

'I don't stopwatch my life.'

'You can't estimate roughly?'

'That's right, I can't.'

'Did any of the hotel staff speak to you when you got back?'

'Only the clerk at the desk who gave me my key.'

'Perhaps he will be able to say at what time you returned?'

'How am I supposed to know what he will or will not be able to do?'

'What clothes were you wearing that night? Were they the ones you have on now?'

'If they were, you'd know without having to ask.' He stood, walked over to the table, poured himself another drink. 'You obviously think I had something to do with Gaspari's death. Doesn't matter I'd never even met him and so couldn't have the slightest reason to kill him. It's suspicious that I went out for a meal instead of putting up with the pap the hotel reckons the tourists want; it's suspicious I didn't drive straight back; it's suspicious I put on clean clothes. You just have to complicate the simplest bloody thing.'

Alvarez sighed. 'My superior chief is sometimes of the same opinion, but in truth I prefer things to be as simple as possible. Yet sometimes . . .' He shrugged his shoulders. 'Señor, a moment ago you said you couldn't have any reason to kill Señor Gaspari. That is not true and you had a very strong motive for his murder.'

'More complications? You'll have to let me into their secret and brief me on what was this very strong motive.'

'Revenge for your father's death.'

'That presumption might at least have the benefit of mistaken logic if I could be certain where and how my father died. But I can't. For all I know, he may have left here and travelled to France and it was there, as the official report says, that he died.'

'He did not die in France.'

'How can you be so certain?'

'I have seen his grave on this island.'

Armitage stared at Alvarez. He said, his voice low: 'Is that why you asked me what his initials were?'

'Yes.'

He spoke with sudden violence. 'Then why didn't you bloody well explain why you wanted to know?'

'Because it was impossible and it is only Señor Gaspari's death which has made it possible.'

'That sounds like a load of crap.'

'Sadly, it is the truth . . . If you discovered the grave before I did, then you had a very strong motive for murdering Señor Gaspari.'

'Where is the grave?'

'Immediately outside the cemetery in Bassa Gris.'

'I told you, I was flung out of there by a blimpish colonel before I learned anything.'

'It would not have been difficult to persuade a soldier to search for you. And since Señor Gaspari was almost certainly involved in your father's death . . .'

'How the bloody hell am I supposed to have known that?'

'You suspected it or you would not have tried to break into his house.'

'How many more times do I have to tell you that I didn't?'

Alvarez spoke sadly. 'Señor, every time you lie to me, I lose a little more faith in you.'

'You've one hell of a warped sense of humour! Faith in me, when you're accusing me of murder?'

'I have not accused you because I am still struggling to understand the truth. And I hope very much that the truth will show you did not kill either Señor Gaspari or Pedro Segui.'

'Do I thank you for such generous broad-mindedness?'

'Perhaps I have chosen the wrong words; I often do. What I am trying to say is . . .' He came to a stop, thought for a moment, then continued, speaking very earnestly. 'I am a simple man, señor, and because of this it happens that when

I meet someone, sometimes I like him immediately and instinctively and not because I ask myself questions about him and decide the answers are right. When I like someone and he needs help, then even if he has not asked me to give it to him, I try to do so. Perhaps I make myself sound like someone who wishes to make others think him a better man than he is, but I am not trying to do that. It is the way of the peasant because in the past he has suffered such hardships that friendship was one of the very few pleasures he was allowed to know . . . When I first met you, I instinctively liked you. But because I am a policeman, it was my job to uncover facts and these have implicated you in lies and perhaps in murder. The tighter they have implicated you, the more help you have needed and the more I have wanted to give it and prove their implications wrong. I am certain that the truth must help me do this. Yet each time I ask you to tell me the truth, you lie; every time you lie, it becomes more difficult for me to believe that my instincts were right.'

Armitage drained his glass. 'You're not a policeman, you're a . . . God knows what the hell you are! First class at conning a man into talking . . . All right, confession time. I did try to break into that house. But when the alarms went off, I was scared into next week and I took off at a rate of knots.'

'Why did you try to break in?'

'Because I was dumb enough to believe I might find something inside that would answer all the questions.'

'Why should you have thought that?'

'Isn't it all too obvious?'

'It was because of what you had learned from the señora?'

'I've already told you that she just couldn't understand the basis of the relationship between Gaspari and her father and why they'd remained friends over so many years. Gaspari was crude in every way—not only had he made a pass at her, he'd tried to get her to watch pornographic tapes. Yet her father hated crudity and bad manners . . .

People of very different likes and dislikes can be friendly and in a foreign country nationals can be drawn together even though they'd not want to know each other in their own, but I got it into my head that this unlikely friendship might hold the key to their relationship with my father—assuming there had been any sort of a one. I was going to search Gaspari's place . . . God knows what I really expected to find.'

'Have you ever been inside his house?'

'Never.'

'There is one last thing, señor, and then I will go. I would like to have a set of your fingerprints.'

'Why?'

'So that they can be compared with any prints that are found inside Señor Gaspari's house.'

'I tell you, I've never been inside.'

'Then you need not fear that if any prints are found, they will prove to be yours. If you will come down to my car, I have the equipment there.'

'With all your talk of wanting to help me, you don't stop thinking I may have murdered the old man, do you?'

'I am a detective and so I cannot let my liking blind me to my duty.'

'It seems like a case of heads you win, tails I bloody lose.'

CHAPTER 19

Alvarez crossed the dining-room to the sideboard, bent down and opened one of the doors. There was a shout. 'Is that you, Enrique?' Hastily, he closed the door, straightened up, and went through to the kitchen.

Dolores, who stood by the table, had a pestle in her right hand. 'Cousin Francisca phoned.' She picked up four teeth of skinned garlic and dropped them into a mortar, began to work the pestle. 'She's invited us all to lunch on Sunday and says she's going to cook lechona to her mother's old recipe. But don't start getting any wrong ideas.'

'About what?'

'She's a family woman and very kind-hearted. That's why she's cooking lechona, not because of anything else.'

'What on earth are you getting at?'

'You know very well. Pass me the olive oil.'

He crossed to the nearest cupboard and brought out a bottle of virgin oil—Dolores insisted on the finest ingredients. She thanked him with a brief nod of the head, slightly increased her rate of working. 'She's a woman of much taste. So try not to speak too crudely.'

'When do I ever do that?'

'Most of the time, like all men.'

'Then since she was married, she'll be used to crude talk.'

'Don't be stupid.'

'If you're so worried about how I'm going to behave, why did you accept the invitation for me?'

'Because she's going to all the trouble of cooking what happens to be your favourite meal.'

'Have you even stopped to think that maybe she doesn't see me in quite such a bad light as you do?'

'She's an intelligent woman,' Dolores said dismissively.

Alvarez returned to the dining-room and went over to the cupboard, poured himself a large drink. It did not exactly boost morale to have one's cousin so freely and unnecessarily critical about one's social manners . . . Could Dolores be suffering from jealousy? Women were so often illogical that one could never be certain what their reactions would be. She deeply loved everyone in the family—did she now stupidly fear that perhaps some of the love that she was given in return was about to be lost to another? There was no true relationship between himself and 'Cousin' Francisca, so would it possibly be more than mere coincidence which had prompted her to cook his favourite meal? . . . There were times when perhaps his manners and speech might be termed crude, but then the islanders had always been robust. And come to that, he'd caught a look in her eyes which suggested that there might be a time and an occasion when, far from being repelled by crudity, she would respond to it . . . Just as a matter of pure interest, it would be an idea to find out if the old man who owned the field next to Ca'n Pyloto really did want to sell . . .

Alvarez parked to the side of the lean-to garage and walked round to the front door of Ca Na Florina. He knocked.

Scalfaro greeted him in his fluent if accented Spanish and led the way through to the sitting-room. Alvarez expressed his regrets at Señor Gaspari's death.

Scalfaro said sadly: 'The young think that the older one becomes, the easier it is to accept death. That just isn't true: the older one is, the more one longs for immortality. The death of a friend is twice a tragedy because it proves that immortality is unobtainable . . . What will you drink?'

Once he'd served the drinks and was seated, Scalfaro raised his glass. 'To those of us who are left.'

'Senor, I regret I have to tell you that it is possible that Señor Gaspari did not die accidentally.'

'You're saying he may have been murdered? My God!'

'So now I have to discover whether this is so and then, if it is, to identify the murderer.'

'I suppose you do . . . That sounds stupid. But what you've just said has really shaken me.' He drank. 'Are you sure you're right? I mean, who could want to murder Giovanni?'

'I am hoping you will be able to answer that question.'

'My answer has to be a flat denial. Nobody could have wished him dead. He'd become almost a hermit after his wife's death and apart from me, saw almost no one. How could anyone have a motive for killing him? Or was he killed in the course of a burglary? It's only a short time ago when there was that attempt to break into his place.'

'The motive almost certainly couldn't have been theft. I believe it must lie in the past. Señor, both you and he were granted residencias in nineteen forty-four on the order of the Governor-General; they were perpetual, so have never had to be renewed. I have not before heard of similar residencias and nor has anyone working in the Ministry. Will you tell me why the Governor-General, who normally would never have concerned himself in such a matter, should have agreed to your being granted something which may well be unique?'

'I'm afraid I can't.'

'You can't or you won't?'

'Can't.'

'Because bureaucrats feel obliged to make notes about everything and, having made them, are loath to destroy them even when it clearly would be better to do so, there are handwritten notes attached to the forms relating to the original granting of the residencias. These state that the names by which you and Señor Gaspari are now known are false.'

Scalfaro drank. 'You've dug very deeply.'

'Do you agree that your true name is not Scalfaro?'

'Under Spanish law, it is.'

'And under Italian law?'

'I'm afraid I'm not certain.'

'What was your birth name?'

'The authorities promised I'd never have to divulge it.'

'They could not know that almost fifty years later Señor Gaspari would be murdered.'

'Are you saying that the murder—which you appear to accept as fact now— negates the promise made then?'

'It has to.'

'A promise is never more than conditional?'

'Politics is founded on such assumption . . . Señor, what was your name in Italy?'

Scalfaro raised his glass, drained it. He stood. 'I think in English it is called Dutch courage; no doubt, in Holland it is called English courage. Whatever the true name, my resolve needs to be bolstered by another drink. You'll join me, even though I suspect you're a man whose resolve never needs boosting?'

Alvarez passed his glass. Scalfaro left, returned to hand it to him refilled. 'Your born name, señor?'

'Filippo Nicolazzi.'

'Why was your name changed with the authority of the Governor-General?'

'Not only was the promise made that I would never be obliged to divulge the details, I, in turn, swore never voluntarily to give them.'

'You have no option and therefore are absolved from your oath.'

'A Jesuitical argument, surely? . . . I remember that on a previous occasion I told you a very little about my early life; when the details differ now from those I gave previously, please remember that I felt constrained to change or omit facts in order to hold to my original oath. Honour dishonourably maintained, I suppose one could say.

'My parents lived for the present and to hell with the future. That's not a criticism, merely a statement of fact. Had my father ever considered the future, he would have accepted that his talent as an actor did not match his enthusiasm and so he would have obtained a regular, pensionable job—he was possessed of considerable intelligence, except where his own interests were concerned. Unfortunately, throughout his career he was convinced he was just about to score such a resounding triumph on the stage that he would irresistibly be lifted among the stars and therefore he considered that to turn his back on acting would be a betrayal of the Italian stage. My mother, who was a better actress than he was actor, never destroyed this belief because to have done so would have been to destroy him; that was why she gave up acting except when the need for money became really desperate.

'All my early years were spent travelling from country town to country town, with stopovers in villages when times were unusually hard. When old enough I became assistant stage manager, unpaid of course, and when necessary I appeared on the stage. I don't think I was a particularly poor actor, but nobody ever suggested I was destined for greater things. By the time I was eighteen, I had travelled most of rural Italy, I could recite passages from dozens of melodramatic plays—in those days, the provincials liked stark passion and gore—and from a few good ones, I had learned how to persuade creditors to accept less than the bills they presented, and how to steal a meal when that was essential . . . I was a veteran of life with no roots and no friends.

'Politics was a discipline for which my father had the greatest contempt—perhaps because a deputy had once tried to seduce my mother while offering the chance of a short season in Rome as the bait to engage my father's blind eye. Being a man who seldom saw any reason for keeping his thoughts to himself, he never hesitated to discuss the failings of contemporary politicians. Il Duce did not encourage such Philistine behaviour and one night my father was beaten by several thugs; he died the next morning. My mother died months later from a broken heart, a complaint dismissed by the medical profession, thereby proving how much they still have to learn.

'I was left with one suit out of which I had unquestionably grown, a small handful of lire, and a host of memories of disorganized happiness. I had to live, so I searched for a job. I became an unskilled worker in a textile factory in Prato. We made vests. From the day I left that factory, I have never worn a vest.

'I wasn't an aggressive person and so it didn't occur to me to volunteer to join the forces and I waited until the decision was made for me. For some reason they gave me the chance to join the navy—an enviable choice since it was a recognized fact that the Italian captains preferred to be in port rather than at sea. I was posted to the *Altamura*, an ancient cruiser which dated from the First World War. In many ways, it was a good posting. Twice our squadron was ordered out to engage the enemy and twice we suffered grave mechanical failure in the engine-room that prevented us leaving port. On each occasion, we clubbed together to give the engine-room staff a party.

'The bulkheads of the *Altamura* were always running with condensation, the air-conditioning seldom worked, and the captain disliked looking down from his eyrie and seeing the weather decks cluttered up with ordinary seamen who weren't working, so all our off-duty time had to be spent below. I, along with others, went down with TB and was shipped ashore and into hospital, much to the chagrin of our unfortunate shipmates who remained healthy.

'I was discharged at the end of 'forty-two and put on light duties; these turned out to be acting as a factotum at a rest centre not far from Genoa where naval officers recuperated after the stresses brought about by trying to keep out of range of the British navy. One of the officers there was Lieutenant Count Alfredo Capria, decorated for bravery so often that there was hardly room on his chest for all the ribbons. He was wealthy, patriotic, and condescendingly pleasant to his inferiors except when drunk.

'We got on remarkably well since, with my experience, I could put on an act. I radiated awed deference and complimented him whenever possible, which pleased him no end. When he left, he gave me a very handsome tip. Most of the officers were more likely to try to borrow money than to give it. I continued at the rest centre, moulding my character to whatever it was expected to be.

'The Count returned to the base in 'forty-three, four days after I'd received a new posting to a destroyer. He said how glad he was to find me still there, eager to meet his every need. I sadly confessed that I would not for long be able to enjoy the privilege since I had received my posting. He told me to tear it up. Naturally, I asssumed he was drunk. He wasn't. The day before I had been due to depart, the posting was cancelled and I was informed that henceforth I was under the Count's, and only the Count's orders.

'Two weeks later he told me to get packed and be ready to move at an hour's notice. He didn't say why or where to and I didn't ask because the first rule of survival in any service is not to ask questions. In the event, a car took us down the coast to Genoa and there we boarded a submarine together with four other hands.

'I've always suffered from claustrophobia, but naturally no one in the navy was the slightest bit interested in that. During daylight, the sub stayed below, during darkness she sailed on the surface, but we weren't allowed above even for a couple of minutes to get a breath of fresh air. I suffered such fear it was a wonder my hair didn't turn white and fall out. My hammock was slung over one of the spare torpedoes and for a while I even considered bringing my ordeal to an end by giving the detonator a wallop . . . After endless time—I think it was four days—we arrived at our destination and I learned for the first time that I and the four others were relieving men at a base, commanded by the Count, which serviced and refuelled submarines working the western Mediterranean. The base was in Llueso Bay.'

It took Alvarez several seconds to accept the significance of what he'd just heard. Then he murmured: 'Sweet Mary!'

'Quite! When Spain was officially neutral, she was assisting one of the belligerents and had been almost from Italy's declaration of war in the middle of nineteen-forty.'

The facts slowly arranged themselves in Alvarez's mind. During the Civil War, Italy had supported the Nationalists. Later, when they themselves had become directly involved in war, they had called on Spain to repay their favour. The Spanish government, far too wily openly to support the Axis too soon, had agreed to give secret assistance—thereby making a mockery of their declared neutrality. At the time, it must have seemed an astute move since it seemed the Axis must win and they would undoubtedly remember their friends. But the course of the war had changed and the Italians had been defeated in Africa, Sicily had been conquered, and Mussolini had resigned; Italy had changed sides and it had become clear to most that both Germany and Japan must eventually be beaten. That move could now be seen to have been not astute, but very dangerous . . . After the end of the war, every possible effort had been made to conceal what had happened—not only because of the damaging practical effects that publication of the facts would have, but also because a Spaniard was a man who, however poor in worldly goods, was always rich in pride— and what pride would be left to those who belonged to a nation which had been guilty of such duplicity? As Korinjora's tribe knew, time changed everything, even the grains of sand in the desert. Italy, along with Germany and Japan, had regained her place among the honourable nations of the world, democracy had come to Spain, the war had become only a bitter memory to those who'd suffered it and another piece of boring history to those who had not; hatred and revenge were forgotten. But one thing that time had trouble in changing was pride—pride could never be re-trieved easily. No wonder so much pressure had been placed on him to drop the case . . .

'What happened while you were there?'

'We landed and took over the running of the base which was set around a small, deepwater cove in Bassa Gris, almost hidden from the rest of the bay. We worked and lived in limbo. None of the crew of any submarine was ever allowed ashore and I remember one boat which arrived with a case of suspected acute appendicitis. A request for a Spanish doctor to see him was refused and he had to sail off—I suppose the poor devil died at sea. Our complex was surrounded by two rings of barbed wire with roughly ten metres between them. No-man's land, we called that gap, not without a certain irony. Beyond the second ring were Spanish guards with orders to shoot anyone who tried to cross the land in either direction. Every possible precaution was taken to prevent anyone learning what was going on.'

Alvarez remembered something until now long since for-gotten. Many years ago he'd spoken to an old, retired

fisherman, half blind and crippled by arthritis. The fisherman had told him that a little while after the war (he'd
meant the Civil War; for all elderly Spaniards, that was the
benchmark in time that the Second World War was for
other Europeans) there had been a period when the military
had disturbed the lives of countless people without giving
any explanation. Families had been forcibly moved from
the port; fishermen had been forbidden to work in Llueso
Bay and had had to fish in Puerta Nueva Bay, which had
led to violent rows and even one pitched battle with the
locals; farmers had even been forbidden to take their mule
carts down to the beach at the beginning of the year to
collect the seaweed which they needed to fertilize their
land . . .

'The Count,' continued Scalfaro, 'worked me a sight
harder than he did himself. I had to keep the logs, check
the stores, and even decode the endless radio messages
which as often as not were vitally unimportant. We lived in
one small house, the other four in an even smaller one. The
Count was forever complaining that it was a pigsty, but for
me it was a luxurious villa because for the first time since
joining the navy I had a room to myself. If cockroaches
played football throughout the night, I was a good sleeper.

'To begin with, the base had proved to be a great success,
but not long before I arrived, a boat was lost soon after
sailing. She was followed by two more. People began to talk
about some sort of breach of secrecy. Far fewer boats called
in and soon we didn't have much more to do than sit out
in the sun, stare across the bay, and try to remember what
girls looked like. Then came Sicily. The panic that caused
turned to chaos when Il Duce was forced to resign. And
when it became clear that Italy was going to change sides,
the Spanish authorities ordered us to close down the base
and vanish, PDQ.

'We asked for a sub to come and pick us up, but it
was some time before anyone at home would take the
responsibility of organizing our collection. Finally, however,

one Sunday, a boat arrived just after midnight. I'd pinched some tablets from the medical store which were supposed to knock one right out and I reckoned that if I remained unconscious until we were in sight of Italy, I might retain my sanity. Then, a quarter of an hour before we were due to board, all documents destroyed, all stores loaded, the Count casually informed me that we two weren't returning. We were leaving the base by land to go to another part of the island. I was in such a state of nerves that I ignored the first rule of survival and asked him why we weren't going back in the boat. "There's every chance that the submarine will be attacked and destroyed," was his reply. Needless to say, that dropped my blood pressure down to zero. "Further," he went on, "if you return, you'll be transferred to the army, since there's precious little navy left, and you'll be given a rifle and told to fire it at the other side, whichever is the other side by then. You'll be cold, wet, and hungry, and your life expectancy will be measured in days rather than weeks. If a miracle happens and you survive, you'll find yourself living in a country that's shattered and will take years to recover. Without skills, money, or influence, you'll remain at the bottom of the pile, even after recovery begins. You and poverty will remain boon companions. On the other hand, if you stay here with me, you will be living in a country which is already on the road to recovery and you will have an income that will enable you to lead the life of a gentleman."

'I wasn't certain whether I was being ordered or bribed to stay. Anyway, I stayed and the boat left without me. I believe it was, in fact, sunk. We left the camp one night by car and were driven to Palma. We lived in a hotel for several months and then he told me he'd bought two houses, one for him, one for me, and he would be giving me the money to have mine reformed. Not long after I moved in, I met Lucía and we married and had Nicola. And the rest of the story, you already know.'

Alvarez thought for a moment. 'Señor, you have told me

much, but not enough. Clearly, it was on the orders of the Governor-General that you were allowed to stay on the island, but why were you given such permission?'

'I can't answer that, any more than I can answer all the other questions to which you want answers. You've got to remember that originally I was a rating, obeying orders and I was never quite certain when, or even if, that relationship came to an end. Things happened, and as a man who'd learned to keep his head down, I just accepted them.'

'Yet you must have been curious?'

'Of course. But every time I felt my curiosity becoming keen enough to become embarrassing, I reminded myself that I was leading the life of a gentleman and I killed that curiosity because he was not a man to welcome opposition in any shape or form.'

'Where does your money come from?'

'The Count might not have been the most democratic of men, but he was a man of his word. Every week he handed me a large sum in cash; in fact, he's been so generous that I've been able to travel quite a bit.'

'And now?'

'That, as the Americans used to say, is the sixty-four-thousand dollar question.' Scalfaro finished his drink. 'Unless he's left me something in his will—and I've no reason to believe that he has—my income has obviously come to an abrupt end. It's a possibility I've been considering . . . You are curious as to my conclusions? I'm a very prudent man because my parents taught me the price of improvidence. I never spent all the money the Count gave me, despite my travels, so now I have some capital. Once I've sorted things out, I will sell this house—which is now worth very much more than was paid for it—and I'll return to Italy. If I choose one of the poorer parts of the country, the house I buy will cost considerably less than this one will sell for and the difference can be added to my existing capital. I hope then to have enough to lead a reasonable life. And when I need a little excitement—if, as I sincerely hope, Nicola marries Steven—I will still have somewhere to travel to which I can afford.'

'It would seem that Señor Gaspari's death has unfortunate repercussions as far as you're concerned.'

'Surely, still more for himself?' Scalfaro stood. 'I have bored you for far too long and my throat is dry from talking. Let me get you another drink.' He took Alvarez's glass and left.

When he returned, Alvarez said: 'Perhaps you don't know why you were allowed to stay here with the obvious blessing of the Governor-General, but you must have formed some idea why Señor Gaspari wanted you to stay and why he gave you considerable sums of money over the years?'

'Naturally I've asked myself those questions many times. I've always come up with the same answers. He was not from an ancient and noble family, but an upstart one, and he was so conscious of that fact that it made him very insecure—ridiculous, really, when he had all the security of a fortune. Because he was insecure, he was always suspicious that anyone who was friendly had a mercenary motive. Being of a dour character anyway, it was very difficult for him even to begin to make any friends; add to that the fact that he was the complete xenophobe and insisted on telling every Spaniard he met how much better things were ordered in Italy and you'll realize that—since very few Italians live on this island—even if a friendship did begin, it did not last. So he needed companionship, as opposed to the relationship one has with a woman, and he recognized that he'd only find this with someone of his own nationality whom he could despise, but who, even if this contempt were recognized, would never turn against him. As for me, life's taught me that pride takes second place to eating.' He could not hide a certain self-contempt.

'You wrong yourself, señor. At first, surely you were in a position where you had no option but to accept events. Once you had a choice, would you not have been very foolish to reject his offer? Most employers buy a little of the employees' pride.'

Alvarez parked outside Sa Serra, unlocked the front door, and went inside. He wondered how he could ever have overlooked the need to discover whether Gaspari had made a will.

One of the two spare bedrooms had been used as an occasional office and a chest-of-drawers contained papers, not clothes. It became clear that Gaspari had been a man who seldom, if ever, threw anything away. The Spanish cheque-book stubs, bank statements, currency receipts, household receipts, and copies of tax declarations dated back for years. There were photocopies of past applications for a Spanish driving licence, carbon copies of business letters—one of these was to a bank in Liechtenstein, asking them to buy forward dollars; he made a note of the address— service manuals for domestic equipment. But no will.

Downstairs, he checked in the telephone directory and found that there was one solicitor in Meranitx. He telephoned the number, spoke to Señor Llabres, identified himself and the reason for making the call.

'I think I drew up a will for the señor, but it would have been a long time ago so I'll have to check. Hang on, will you?'

He waited.

'Yes. The will's dated some twenty-five years ago and, naturally, was registered in Madrid.'

'Will you tell me briefly what the details are?'

'Señor Gaspari leaves everything of which he is possessed at the time of death to his cousin. In the event of his cousin's predeceasing him, then to his cousin's children.'

'Does it list his possessions?'

'No.'

'So there's no reference to any holdings in Liechtenstein?'

'None.'

'What's the cousin's name and address?'

'Franca Darida, Twenty-three, Viale Carducci, Fidenag-giore, Tuscany.'

'Will you give me the reference number of the will so that I can check with Madrid if it's still valid?'

Llabres gave a number.

Alvarez thanked him and rang off. If this twenty-five-year-old will were valid, then Scalfaro not only did not benefit from Gaspari's death, he actively suffered loss because of it. So he had no motive for the murder; only Armitage did.

CHAPTER 20

It occurred to Alvarez, just before he'd intended to ring Palma to discover if the lab had yet checked the prints on the glass, that among all the papers in the chest-of-drawers there had not been a single statement or cheque-book stub from a bank in Liechtenstein. Yet Gaspari had clearly been a man who had obsessively kept all records and it seemed reasonable to suppose that he would have wanted to know how his balance stood. Did banks who operated with great secrecy not provide statements? Perhaps Gaspari had requested that none was ever sent in order to make certain that this account never came to the eyes of the prying tax authorities? Yet by changing in his Maranitx bank notably large cheques on the Liechtenstein bank—for the moment he assumed that the account had been held in the same bank he had asked to buy forward dollars—he had exposed the presence of the account to anyone who investigated his financial affairs . . . It was a tiny and probably meaningless point, but it niggled. Superior Chief Salas would no doubt have told him that it niggled because he had a tiny and essentially meaningless mind . . .

He telephoned the fingerprint section of the Institute of Forensic Sciences.

'No, we haven't yet had time to carry out tests on the glass you sent us. We do have other work, you know.'

He said he did realize that and rang off. He decided he'd obtain copies of Gaspari's will and preliminary death certificate and fax these through to Liechtenstein and ask for details of the account on the grounds that such details were needed in connection with implementing the will.

There was a phone call on Friday morning from the Franziskaner Bank. Herr Aubert introduced himself as director of current accounts. He spoke Spanish fluently and with so little accent that only an occasional word betrayed him as a foreigner. 'The copies of the death certificate and will you sent by fax aren't sufficient authority, I'm afraid, but certified copies, properly notarized, will be. When we have those, monies will be released.'

'Can you tell me what's now in the deceased's account, what levels deposits have been running at, if any large amount has recently been withdrawn and, if so, to whom it was paid? Also, what other business you've done with him?'

'I think I can answer most of that, given the faxed copies. There is just the one account and at no time has there been a large balance, consequently, no large amount has recently been withdrawn. The account's profile is that each week money has been paid in and two or three days later, withdrawn, leaving only a buffer to make certain the account remains active.'

'What sort of money are we talking about?'

'Two thousand Swiss francs.'

'And it's always the same amount?'

'That is withdrawn as is paid in, yes. But over the years the amount in question has increased, almost certainly to match inflation.'

'Isn't it a bit odd—always paying in and then almost immediately drawing out?'

'Not at all. This account has obviously been used as a "postbox".'

'What's that mean?'

'The main account is held elsewhere; the postbox account is fed regular, relatively small amounts.'

'Why go through all this runaround?'

There was a dry chuckle. 'It sounds, Inspector, as if you are not a man who has cause to hide the source of his capital! Rich men need, however, to do so and that's why banks with financial security are so attractive to them. But due to diplomatic and commercial pressures from countries such as America, it is becoming more accepted that the books of such banks should be opened up where evidence can be supplied that the money has a criminal source; in most countries, tax evasion is a criminal offence. The postbox inserts an extra layer of security. Because you have sufficient authority, I have given you details of the account. But if you were now thinking of asking me to name the source of the money paid into this account, I would have to disappoint you and say I must refuse the information.'

'There is almost certainly a criminal element.'

'That makes no difference. If you wish to force disclosure of details of the account with this other bank, you must present the proof of a criminal element to them, not me.'

'Until I know their nationality and name, I can't do that.'

'Precisely why the postbox system is so popular.'

'To an innocent like me, that seems to be making a nonsense of any agreement to disclose details of an account with criminal connections.'

Another dry chuckle. 'Quite so! But commerce is usually ahead of the law.'

Alvarez realized that he was remarkably naïve concerning the lives the rich lived.

He telephoned the Institute of Forensic Sciences again, late in the afternoon.

'Yeah, we've checked out the glass now. Two sets of prints, one of which matches the comparison prints.'

Alvarez lit a cigarette and smoked, staring unseeingly

through the open window at the sun-blasted wall of the house opposite. Armitage claimed he'd never set foot inside Gaspari's house, yet his prints were on the glass that had been on the draining-board in the kitchen, almost certainly placed there to conceal the fact that a second person had been present.

He telephoned Palma and said to the secretary with a plum in her mouth that he'd like a word with Superior Chief Salas. There was a long wait before she said: 'The superior chief is exceedingly busy. What is it you want?'

'To report the latest developments in the Gaspari case.'

'What are they?'

'I think it would be best if I speak to him personally.'

'Wait,' she snapped, piqued by his refusal to tell her.

There was an even longer wait before she said: 'The superior chief will arrange for Commisario Orifla to be at the post at nine tomorrow morning. You are to report to him.'

As he replaced the receiver, he thought that there really wasn't much difference between a millionaire trying to protect his assets and a superior chief trying to protect his position; both made use of a postbox.

Orifla had the useful knack of being able to alter his projected image (though sometimes at the cost of clarity of speech) when circumstances made this a rewarding thing to do. He shook hands with Alvarez, said that it really was a fine day (hardly remarkable in the middle of the hottest and driest summer for years) and expressed his satisfaction that it was Alvarez who was in charge of a difficult case because that ensured that the investigations were efficiently, diplomatically, and painstakingly carried out.

'Señor, since Señor Gaspari was murdered . . .'

'You raise a very relevant point. As the post-mortem results are not through, can we yet be certain it was murder?'

'I've had a word with Professor Fortunato's assistant who unofficially confirms that it was.'

'I see.'

'Since then, I've learned certain facts which—well, which make it clear why the authorities have been trying so hard to stifle the investigations.'

'That is a ridiculous claim and one you should know better than to make,' said Orifla, careful to speak more in sorrow than in anger.

'I only wish it were ridiculous . . . Señor Gaspari and Señor Scalfaro were given false names before their perpetual residencias were issued and their original names were Count Alfredo Capria and Filippo Nicolazzi. Both men were in the Italian navy, one an officer, the other a rating, and at the beginning of nineteen-forty-three, Nicolazzi was brought by submarine to Llueso Bay to relieve the team of Italians, commanded by Count Capria, who serviced and replenished the stores of Italian submarines operating from Bassa Gris.'

Orifla's voice was high. 'For God's sake, man, do you know what you're saying? That has to be arrant nonsense.'

'I have every reason to believe it is fact.'

'Impossible. Spain was neutral.'

'Which was why the secrecy was so great. If the records are checked, it will be discovered that for some reason, then unknown to the locals, families were moved away from the port and farmers weren't even permitted to gather seaweed at the beginning of the year.'

'I don't want to hear any more of this.'

'I very much regret, señor, that since we are investigating the murder of Señor Gaspari and these facts form the background, you must hear it all. Señor Armitage's father was in the British navy. Clearly, the Italian submarine base was not the complete secret the Italians believed and the British had got wind of it. Señor Perry Armitage, who spoke Spanish like a native, was sent to the island to discover the truth about it. He must have learned that Pedro was allowed into the base and questioned him to discover what was going on . . . Something went wrong and his true identity was discovered. One must assume that as a consequence he was executed as a spy.

'The war slowly swung in the Allies' favour. Now, naturally, the Spanish authorities wanted to be friendly with the winning side; while the British were very conscious of what effect it would have on Spanish pride to learn that they had been spied upon. So it suited both sides to conceal the truth. In Spain, the death of Perry Armitage wasn't acknowledged; in England, he was decorated as an undercover hero who had been captured and executed in France. And once the truth was hidden, it was very much more comfortable for both sides if it remained so; paradoxically, though, the longer it was, the more explosive its disclosure could prove to be. It would have remained hidden to this day had not Señor Steven Armitage discovered a letter written to his mother.'

'And the Englishman . . . He knows all this?'

'I can't say. If Señor Armitage does, then obviously he had a very strong motive for Señor Gaspari's murder.'

'Who else had a motive?'

'The only other person whom it is conceivable might have had one is Señor Scalfaro. I've checked his financial affairs, but since Señor Gaspari was providing him with his only income and that income has ceased with death, then it was entirely in his interests for Señor Gaspari to outlive him.'

'You are telling me that Armitage has to be the murderer.'

'I suppose so. More especially since although he denies ever having been in Señor Gaspari's house, his fingerprints were on a glass which was used on the night of the murder.'

'Why haven't you arrested him?'

'There certainly seems to be sufficient, perhaps more than sufficient evidence. But . . .'

'What?'

'There are one or two inconsistencies.'

Orifla brought his silver cigarette case from his coat pocket and did not offer it. He lit a cigarette. When he next spoke, it was clear he had decided to resume his normal identity. 'Superior Chief Salas had a word with me last night during which he again made the point that you are a man for whom a complication is a perverse pleasure. You are seemingly incapable of understanding that most crime is straightforward and therefore needs to be view straightforwardly. Perceived apparent inconsistencies are far more likely to be a reflection of the investigator's incompetence than of any importance.'

'I'm certain that's normally correct, señor, but . . .'

'Why are there always "buts" where you are concerned?'

'It's just that there have been times when a small inconsistency has turned out to be so important that it has thrown an entirely new light on a case.'

'Then your investigation prior to such an incident was clearly inefficient.'

'I'm not sure that that necessarily follows.'

'I am.'

'Señor, something tells me that we do not yet know the full facts of this case.'

'If so, there is only one man to blame.'

'But I've only just been able to learn one or two things which may be important.'

'For example?'

'Señor Gaspari had an account with a bank in Liechtenstein, but among his papers there are no statements or cheque-stubs from that bank. A man as careful to keep records as he must surely be expected to file both . . .'

'In your many years of work, have you really never learned that it is a serious mistake to assume a person will at all times behave in a logical manner?'

'Surely, when it comes to keeping financial records . . .' Alvarez shrugged his shoulders. 'Señor, I would like to have permission to travel to Italy.'

'Why?'

'To try and learn more about Count Capria.'

'What conceivable point is there in that?'

'I don't really know. But I have this feeling that a full understanding of his character could be important.'

'The superior chief also mentioned to me that there are times when you suffer what you are pleased to describe as "feelings". He advised me to discount them completely. I assured him that the advice was unnecessary. I am not a man who believes in "feelings". A trip to Italy is totally unnecessary and therefore out of the question.'

'But if a visit did manage to turn up something important, then surely it would be justified?'

'Are you incapable of appreciating that even were I sympathetic to your proposal, I could never accede to the request when that is dependent for its justification on the request's being granted?'

'Then I'm going to have to arrest Señor Armitage.'

'Of course.'

'But I do not think he really can be the murderer. I can see him killing when he's in a rage, but not planning a murder and committing it in cold blood. He's surely a man of warm, quick emotions, not cool and collected ones.'

'You have a degree in criminal psychology?'

'No, señor.'

'Then leave such judgements to those who have.'

'There is one more point.'

'If it's as vapid as the last, I see no reason to bother to make it.'

'If I arrest Señor Armitage, all the facts in the case will have to come out.'

'The long past is immaterial to the present. The court will hold such evidence to be inadmissible.'

'The press would be very interested in it, though.'

'Are you daring to suggest you would give them such information?'

'Certainly not, señor. But Señor Armitage probably would.'

'According to you, he may well be innocent. If that were

the case, he would know nothing about the more sensitive facts.'

'If he's wrongly charged with murder, he may well become aware of them. Then, of course, he would be keen to divulge them since they militate against his guilt; or at least can be called upon when pleading in mitigation of sentence. Publication of the more damaging facts must inevitably cause severe diplomatic rows—and the fallout from them would affect all of us from the superior chief down. So that's why I thought it might just be worth my while to go to Italy. Admittedly, the chances of discovering anything significant have to be very small, but it did seem—wrongly, as you have pointed out—that in the circumstances even the smallest chance was worth pursuing.'

Orifla leaned forward and stubbed out his cigarette with far more force than was necessary. 'Goddamnit,' he shouted, 'this is the second time you've—' He stopped, just in time. It was hardly fitting that a comisario should admit that he was again about to be blackmailed into doing what his inspector wanted.

Dolores, who was knitting as she watched the television, looked up as Alvarez entered the room. 'You're back very early, Enrique.'

'Yes, I know. That's because there is so much going on.'

The illogicality of that answer escaped her. 'You look tired. They work you much too hard.'

He took that as an encouragement to go over to the sideboard and pour himself a brandy. After adding ice, he sat. The programme came to an end and Dolores finished the row, pushed the knitting to the back of one needle, stuck both needles into the ball of wool, and put wool, needles and knitting, into a linen bag. 'I must go and see how the cooking is getting on. Juan and Isabel are with Julia, so it's only us three and I've made garbanzos Catalán.' She stood.

'By the way, I have to fly to Italy tomorrow.'

'What's that?'

He was unsurprised by her sharp reaction to his news. She worried endlessly about her family when everything proceeded normally; when something unusual happened, she became heir to nameless fears and saw disaster everywhere. 'There's no need to worry,' he said soothingly.

She sounded more angry than worried. 'Are you also returning from Italy tomorrow?'

He smiled. 'Hardly.'

'So will you then be returning early on Sunday morning?'

'Not a chance. I don't expect to be back before Tuesday at the earliest.'

'You are telling me that you will not be here at lunch-time on Sunday?'

'I won't, no. But is that important?'

Her dark brown eyes flashed; her voice sharpened. 'Only a man could be so stupid! Where are your wits? Drowned in alcohol?'

'Here, what's suddenly got you complaining?'

'On Sunday, we are all invited to Cousin Francisca's. I was with her when she bought the whole half side of lechona. I have explained how to make certain that the crackling crackles perfectly. Both of us take all this trouble and then you just stand there and tell me you won't be here?'

'But it's not my fault . . .'

'When has anything ever been any man's fault?'

'But if my work . . .'

She uttered a sound of high disgust, marched into the kitchen where she made a considerable noise as she moved things around.

He drained his glass. Comisario Orifla had made quite a point of the fact that people did not always behave logically. Perhaps he had at some time met Dolores.

CHAPTER 21

Alvarez had by now flown sufficiently frequently to need only three double brandies to dull to the point of resignation his fears of crashing on take-off, losing power on all engines, hitting another plane head-on, being sucked out of his seat in an explosive decompression, being blown up by a terrorist's bomb, running out of fuel, or crashing on landing.

He was met in the arrival lounge by Sergeant Romita, a youngish man with long sideburns and a roving eye, who spoke a Spanish that was frequently larded with French and even the occasional English word.

They left the building and crossed the road to the car park, where a police Fiat had been causing an obstruction next door to the pay-booth. Romita opened the boot and put the suitcase inside. He slammed the lid shut. 'It is a longish drive, so I suggest we stop for a meal in Bellzano. There is a small restaurant there where the food is . . .' He kissed his fingers in a universal gesture of appreciation.

The restaurant was on the corner of one of the many narrow streets in the small town, noted for its glass since the time of the Medici. From the outside, it looked to be little more than a slightly run-down café, but if the furnishings were basic, every table was occupied by people whose contented, glistening features, and in many cases girth, suggested they were connoisseurs of good bourgeois cuisine. One of the young waitresses, a laden tray in her hands, paused long enough to tell them they'd have to wait. Romita awarded Alvarez the rank of superior chief and demanded a table immediately if Italian/Spanish relations were not to be devastated. Another table was somehow edged into a corner of the second dining-room at the rear of the building.

The menu was handwritten and far from extensive, but

Romita swore by Lucullus that every dish was a masterpiece and the gnocchi Bellzano made the gods on Olympus throw aside their ambrosia. Alvarez chose that.

As they waited, they each had a brandy and shared a small earthenware dish of olives. Romita dropped a stone into the ashtray. 'As I said in the car, Franca Darida is quite an important man in Fidenaggiore.'

Alvarez sipped the brandy—slightly heavier than he was used to—put the glass down on the table. There had been an unspoken question in the other's words. 'There's no question that he's in any way mixed up in the case. It's simply that I hope he'll be able to tell me something.'

'That's good. Darida is a man we call . . . I'm not certain how to translate it. He makes certain that everything in town runs smoothly and if he becomes upset, life can become difficult for many.'

'A party boss?'

'You could call him so, but I think that perhaps the only party he truly supports is his own.' Romita smiled, showing very white teeth. 'So what will you be asking him?'

'What kind of person his cousin really was.'

'His cousin? I didn't know he had one.'

'Count Alfredo Capria.'

'A cousin who was a count! I'm sure he wouldn't want that to be generally known since he calls himself a man of the people! . . . Of course, some people lead different lives from others.'

Fidenaggiore was still predominantly Renaissance in style, its most noticeable feature the campanile which predated the church that had been rebuilt after the siege of 1514. The town stood in rich, rolling countryside, noted for its quality hard fruit. The streets were narrow and full of turns and most of the buildings were either four or five floors high. There were three squares and in the largest was the statue, The Two Steeds, presented to the town by Pope Leo XII in 1827 as a tacit and magnanimous admission that his predecessor, Leo X, had been somewhat hasty in ordering the siege of 1514.

Darida's house was on the main square and it faced The Two Steeds. On the ground floor there was a corn and seed merchant with considerable storage area, and access to the living quarters was by stone stairs, their edges worn over the centuries into shallow curves. The walls on either side of the staircase were roughly finished and merely whitewashed and this provided an initial impression of austerity; an impression dispelled when the door at the head of the stairs was opened. The entrance hall was over-furnished in a style that owed more to wealth then taste.

Darida shook hands with exaggerated formality. He was a small, plump man and considering his age his face was remarkably unlined, obviously through great care. His clothes were carefully chosen and very carefully worn. A casual observer might well have placed him as an aged popinjay; Alvarez noted the expression which lurked in the dark brown eyes and decided he could be a very dangerous man.

As soon as they were in the very large sitting-room, even more over-furnished than the entrance hall, he asked them what they would like to drink. Romita translated the question and Alvarez's answer. Darida used a silken bell-pull to summon an eighteen-year-old maid, whose manner was cowed rather than respectful, and told her what to bring. As she left the room, he settled in a large wooden-framed armchair with carved back, sides, and arms, and velvet upholstery; more throne than chair. 'So you are from Mallorca, Inspector? Regrettably, it is not an island I have ever had the good fortune to visit. I fear I cannot afford to travel to faraway places.'

Romita smiled with respectful, amused disbelief.

'So tell me, what can have brought you all the way here?'

'I'd like to talk to you about your cousin, señor.'

'Then you have endured a wasted journey. Both my wife and I are descended from families who lacked the blessing of fecundity and we now find ourselves without a single living blood relative.'

'I'm talking about Count Alfredo Capria.'

'That is a name I have not heard for a long time. I wonder what your interest in him can be since he died so very many years ago?'

'In fact, he died only very recently.'

'He died during the war.'

'No, señor. That death was faked. Further, in his will you are named as the sole beneficiary.'

There was a long silence so that they became aware of the sounds of traffic and people in the square and of the ticking of the very ornate ormolu clock on the marble mantelpiece.

Darida spoke angrily. 'I must presume you have not come all this way merely to be absurd.'

'Far from it.'

'Yet absurd is what you're being. My cousin would not have willingly handed me a crust of bread had he seen me starving in the gutter.'

'You are named in his will.'

'He only ever gave me anything when the giving afforded him a satisfying feeling of contempt. Why should he have acted so out of character?'

'A man can change as he grows older.'

'A leopard cannot change its spots.'

'Nevertheless, it is fact that you inherit his estate.'

'Whatever you say, Alfredo died during the war.'

'Señor, we have undeniable proof that he did not. Tragically, he was murdered last week in Mallorca, under the name of Giovanni Gaspari.'

He stared at Alvarez. 'It seems I have to believe you . . . But even so, I won't accept your description of his murder as tragic.'

The maid returned to the room, carrying a silver salver on which were three crystal goblets. She handed one to each man, careful never to look directly at him, then hurried out.

Darida drank. 'Inspector, you are a man with an express-
ive face and it is obvious that you disapprove of my attitude.
Is that because you subscribe to the belief that the dead
should be sanctified, no matter what, or because you feel I
must be unjustified in my attitude? If the first, there is
nothing I can do but envy you your generous humanity; if
the second, I shall bore you with a little of my family's
history in an effort to justify myself.

'My grandparents had only two children—my mother
and Alfredo's father. My grandfather was an honest, but
poor man—only the poor can afford the luxury of being
honest—until he developed and patented a method of pro-
ducing very high quality glass at half the previous cost. He
then became rich.

'It is a habit of the newly rich to be over-conscious
of their social position and when my mother fell in love
with a worker in one of the glass factories my grandfather
now owned, she was informed that either she called
off the proposed mésalliance or she ceased to be a Capria.
A very determined woman, she chose to marry, thereby
losing both her maiden name and any claim to the family
fortune.

'Alfredo's father never missed a chance. Instead of doing
what he could to help his sister by softening the old man's
absurd attitude, he made certain it was exacerbated. The
old fool never again spoke to my mother.

'We lived within ten kilometres of each other. Two families, related by blood but little else. They were in a vast
mansion, tended by an army of servants, we were in a
humble house and tended by no one; they ate caviar, we ate
pasta; they drank château-bottled, we drank the local wines
which often tasted of old boots.

'The year before the old man died, Alfredo's father married Lucía who came from an ancient family of impeccable
lineage and with fingers in sufficient pies to stock a bakery.
Of small account to either father or son that she lacked both
good looks and a figure. Naturally, when the old man

died, Alfredo's father inherited everything and my mother nothing.

'Lucía, perhaps to compensate for what she saw in the mirror, considered it her duty to meddle in other people's lives by doing good. She decided that I would benefit enormously if I had limited contact with her son because I would thus have the chance to appreciate the refinements that life could offer to those of sufficient breeding to warrant their enjoying them. So three times a week one of the family's limousines driven by one of their chauffeurs came to our village and collected me and took me to their mansion to spend the afternoon with Alfredo. The village lads gave me hell for having rich relatives who, they were convinced, made me think I was better than any of them. They never understood how desperately I envied them for having only poor relatives.

'Just before his death, Alfredo's father was made a count; somehow, a spurious claim to an ancient title was established, undoubtedly aided by the transfer of large sums of money. Lucía demanded that I called Alfredo, Count Alfredo, thereby preparing him for his noble future. For his part, I was Chloe, a miscall that gave him doubled amusement because not only was it feminine, he held it was a diminutive of Cloacina.

'By now you are undoubtedly asking yourself, why did the lad put up with all this? The answer is twofold. He was much larger than I and if I refused to do as he wanted, he beat me up. If I then complained to his mother, he said I was lying and in reality had fallen over and hurt myself and she read me a sanctimonious homily about always telling the truth—even more painful than the beating for ratting on him that he gave me as soon as we were on our own again. Secondly, in order to impress us with her concern for the underprivileged, when I was driven home I was given a hamper of food for the family. My mother had a great liking for luxurious foods, dating from when her father became rich.

'As he grew older, Alfredo became more and more ingenious at making my life a misery. He had all the careless ease of manner of the rich, I had all the awkwardness of the poor, and he never tired of mocking my manners, especially in front of his mother whom he was able to persuade that he was really trying to help me improve myself. He loved practical jokes—setting them, not suffering them—and I cannot begin to count the number of times previously unsuspected buckets of water or filth poured over me. Naturally, he treated me with contempt in front of the servants so that they treated me with an even greater contempt. He'd push me into the swimming pool, knowing I couldn't swim, and he'd stand and jeer as I panicked; then, when he'd finally hauled me out and left me gasping on the edge, he'd dive in and mockingly swim with all the easy grace of someone who was almost of Olympic standard.

'In short, he amused himself at my expense, using envy as a needle, ridicule as a thumbscrew, and contempt as a club . . . Perhaps, Inspector, you can now understand why the news of his murder did not fill me with the sense of shock and horror that one might expect.'

'You obviously had no cause to like him.'

'But not enough to hate him beyond his death? Clearly, you have never had to suffer the persecution of someone who uses every ingenious method that comes to his fertile mind to make your life a living hell.'

'I make no judgement.'

'On the contrary, you judge my hatred.'

Alvarez did not try to argue.

'Have I told you what you wish to know?'

'Just about, señor.'

'And you can now appreciate the kind of man he was?'

He could appreciate what kind of men both the cousins were. 'I understand that in the war he was decorated for bravery?'

'He would always be brave when others could observe

his actions. He lived for the praise of his superiors, the respect of his equals, and the envy of his inferiors.'

'What happened to the estate after the war?'

'It was sold by his wife.'

'By whom?'

'You find the possibility of marriage unlikely? Then I venture to suggest that you have not quite understood the kind of man he was. Alfredo had to conform, so, being rich, he married the daughter of a rich man. Following the family tradition, Beatrice was no beauty; indeed, it would be difficult to say who lacked most, she or Lucía. I was not asked to the wedding, of course. Poor relations are a private amusement.'

'She survived the war?'

'She is, as far as I know, still alive.'

'Do you ever see her?'

'Would you expect me to?'

'Have you any idea where she lives?'

'Off-hand, no. But it is a question which could soon be answered, if needs be. You are intending to visit her in order to acquaint her with the fact that for many years she has not been the widow she believed herself to be? And that her beloved husband has, instead of leaving his estate to her, left it to his despised cousin? How does a proud woman react to such news?' He smiled, satisfied that the contessa would react badly.

CHAPTER 22

The large, elegant villa lay half way up one of the hills which backed the small port of San Stefano. A maid opened the front door. Young and attractive, she immediately caught Romita's interest and he explained at greater length than was necessary who they were.

'I'm not sure the contessa can see you,' she said.

Romita began to translate her answer, but she interrupted him with a flood of Spanish. She was a Filipino and avidly seized the opportunity to speak Spanish. He showed his annoyance; he had become redundant and his standing in her eyes must have suffered.

She changed her mind; perhaps the contessa would after all be able to speak to them. She led the way into a vast sitting-room and said in a low voice: 'Don't be surprised if you find it very difficult to understand her. She's sometimes becoming so confused.' She left.

The room, decorated in light pastel colours, contained several pieces of antique furniture which, in Alvarez's un-qualified judgement, would not have been out of place in a museum; on the walls hung four heavily framed paintings which looked as if they might be Old Masters. He crossed the magnificent Shiraz carpet to the right-hand picture window and stared out. The garden, necessarily of a limited width, was a mass of ordered colour and obviously was looked after by a skilled gardener; beyond its edge, the land sloped away quite steeply and although almost all of the small port was hidden, none of the bay was. Nowhere in the world was more beautiful than Llueso Bay, but he was prepared to admit that with its wooded slopes and complete lack of development, San Stefano Bay ran it a reasonably close second . . .

Contessa Capria entered the room, a stick in her right hand. Darida had suggested that when young she had been strikingly unattractive. Age had exacerbated her physical failings without offering any compensations. Her sense of make-up and dress was extraordinary. Had she been half her age and size, they would still at best have been described as eccentrically oblivious of the facts.

'Good morning. I'm sorry to have kept you waiting so long, but I was resting.' She spoke imperiously, making it clear that the apology was purely formal. She switched from Italian to an easy, but heavily accented, Spanish. 'I understand from Marta that one of you is from Spain?'

'I am, Contessa. Inspector Enrique Alvarez. I live in Mallorca.'

'I was there for a few days several years ago and found it a very beautiful island.' Her tone was distant—the praise was without value. 'Please sit down.' She slowly settled herself on one of the ornate armchairs; she sat very straight-backed. 'Tell me, please, why have you come from Mallorca in order to speak to me?'

'I am investigating a case with which your husband was connected.'

'My husband? But he died a very long time ago.'

'I am afraid that what I have to tell you will come as a severe shock. Your husband did not die during the war as was reported.'

'Of course he did.'

'No, Contessa. He left the navy in nineteen-forty-three, changed his name to Giovanni Gaspari, and lived in Mallorca until last week.'

'That is ridiculous. He died in battle . . .' Abruptly, her gaze became unfocused.

'Your husband did not die until last week.'

She said nothing, indeed gave no indication that she had heard him. Romita shrugged his shoulders. Alvarez said patiently: 'Tragically, he was murdered. Now, I am trying to identify his murderer. You may be able to help me.'

She suddenly turned her head and faced him. 'What is that?' She once more spoke with the sense of authority which she had initially shown.

He repeated what he'd said.

'If it's possible that you are correct, I would imagine he was far too old to be having an affair, but one can never be quite certain. Do you believe it was a jealous husband who killed him?'

'The motive for the murder stems from something that happened during the war which had nothing to do with a jealous husband.'

'Indeed. I often told him that no one ever escapes the

consequences of his acts. He jeered at me for being so naïve as to believe in divine retribution. He was so certain he could do exactly as he wanted and never be made to suffer . . .' Once again, she retreated into her memories. Then, with equal abruptness, as Alvarez was about to speak, she returned from them. 'Was his murder connected with the inquiries made after the war?'

'What inquiries were those?'

'It was when I was living in the flat because my house had been bombed and it was impossible to obtain the materials to have it repaired. It was such a terrible time when there were so few servants and those that there were, were very difficult . . .' She became silent.

Romita said: 'It's hopeless.'

Alvarez ignored him. 'Contessa, what were those inquiries?'

She gave no answer.

He repeated the question, speaking as patiently as ever.

'What inquiries do you keep talking about?'

'The ones concerning your husband that were made after the war.'

'The colonel was an American. He was a nice man.'

'What did he ask you?'

'He wanted to know if Alfredo was truly dead.'

'Why did he ask you that?'

'According to the translator who was a Sicilian . . . Ridiculous, having a Sicilian to translate. One needs a translator to understand a Sicilian.'

'Why did the colonel think your husband might not be dead?'

'He was in the navy.'

'And highly decorated for bravery.'

'I imagine that it was always someone else who was brave and he merely stole the credit,' she said contemptuously.

'Why was the American colonel asking about your husband's service in the navy?'

'He was transferred from general service into Intelligence.

He was very intelligent, but not at all clever. There's a great difference, you know. Had he been clever, he would have understood that eventually one always has to pay. The Church makes that quite clear.'

'Was the colonel interested to hear your husband had been in Intelligence?'

'He knew Alfredo had. It was because of that that he wanted to know about him. He said Alfredo's unit had been guilty of war crimes. They'd captured partisans and tortured them for information. He thought I'd refuse to believe him, but of course I didn't.'

'Why were you ready to believe him?'

'Because Alfredo had always enjoyed being so cruel to me.' She spoke without any visible emotion. 'He was so jealous of me because my family was an ancient one and his had been peasants two generations back; of my manners because they came naturally to me and he had always to remember his. He hated it because his cousin was uncouth; he tried to despise my friends, but couldn't . . . And the only way in which he could get his own back was to humiliate me. He always told me when he'd found a new woman because he knew how much that would hurt. And if I complained, he'd say it was so much more fun to make love to a woman with whom he could bear to leave the light on . . .'

After a while, Alvarez broke the silence. 'Contessa, you and everyone else believed your husband had died during the war. Presumably, the estate became yours?'

'We had no children, so I inherited everything. Except that of his property there was nothing but the house and the land and I had to spend a fortune on repairing the house before I could sell it.'

'Yet surely he was a wealthy man?'

'He was also an intelligent one and had foreseen the war and what the consequences of that would be. He'd moved all his realizable assets abroad.'

'Were you able to trace them?'

'Any such movement of money was illegal, so he'd been very careful there should be no record of what he'd done. If I'd not inherited my father's estate, I would have been so poor . . .' She trailed off into silence. After a moment, she slumped back in the chair, no longer able to, or perhaps bothering to, maintain a straight back.

Alvarez tried once more to gain her attention, but failed. He said to Romita, 'We might as well go.'

'Thank God for that!'

Marta must have been in one of the rooms which had direct access to the hall because as they left the sitting-room, she appeared. Alvarez said that the contessa was obviously very tired and possibly hadn't heard their thanks—would she make certain she passed them on?

They left the villa and returned to the Fiat parked in front of the double garage. Romita settled behind the wheel. 'Half crazy! What a bloody waste of time!'

Alvarez didn't bother to answer that the contessa, unknowingly, had provided him with the last few pieces of information which finally showed where the truth lay.

CHAPTER 23

The information board in the departure hall indicated three-quarters of an hour's delay in the flight to Barcelona. Anything much more than an hour, thought Alvarez, and he'd miss his connecting flight to Palma. He went along to the café at the far end, bought a coffee and a brandy and sat at one of the free tables.

As always, the truth was both obvious and simple when one knew where it lay and how to recognize it. A clever detective would have uncovered and identified it long before he had.

Darida had claimed that leopards never changed their spots. But spots could be camouflaged until they became

very indistinct; indeed, could become part of the camou-
flage. Both the contessa and Darida had painted the character of the dead man in the same colours. A clever (despite
her attempted differentiation between intelligence and
cleverness), jealous, snobbish, sadistic man, yet one who
could, when he wished, present himself as charming, amusing and good company.

Darida's initial reaction to the news that he had been
named sole beneficiary had been one of scornful disbelief.
It had not occurred to him that perhaps the will had been
made to benefit the testator, not the beneficiary. If one man
was the sole inheritor, another could not benefit.

The bank manager in Liechtenstein had explained how
rich men used postbox accounts in order to provide extra
security for their wealth. It had not occurred to him that in
the present case it had been a defence of the income, not
the capital, which had been sought.

It was a common assumption that a man who lived in a
large house was better off than his neighbour who lived in
a small one. A clever man would take advantage of such an
assumption. And if he enjoyed swimming so much that he
wanted a pool, he'd make certain this was built in the
grounds of the large house, not the small one.

A casual interest in pornography was common to many
men when young, but the collecting of it when old was not;
a preference for, or at least a liking of, 'good' music as
opposed to pop, for literature over cheap, trashy fiction, was
usual in those who came from an educated background and
who had themselves had a good education; a wide, upmarket
social background made for a certain ease of manner, a
narrow, downmarket one for an uneasiness which often
manifested itself in surliness . . . On its own, each a gener-
ality which could be dismissed since it was honoured almost
as often in the breach as in the observance; but taken
together, might they not add up to help distinguish between
two men? . . .

Pedro had been simple, so it had been assumed that most

of what he said was simple. Even when he'd made sense, the simplest possible construction had been put on his words. But a good detective would have remembered that what appeared to be simple was not always so. When asked about the base and Perry Armitage, Pedro had named two names. Why immediately assume that he was naming two different men seen at the same time? Why not that he was naming the same man seen at two different times? . . .

Count Alfredo Capria had been clever enough to move the bulk of his fortune in time to save it from the ravages of war. Then what more likely than that he'd have been equally prescient in foreseeing the consequences to himself if the winning Allies learned that he had tortured an Englishman to death in a vain attempt to make him reveal how much he'd discovered and passed on about the secret submarine base in Llueso Bay? Clever men so often made the mistake of seeking clever solutions to their problems, ignoring the fact that there must be times when mundane ones would be more advantageous . . .

Alvarez returned home at 7.15 in the evening. Dolores greeted him with such emotion that it was obvious she had dreaded he never would return. Jaime grinned with pleasure as he indicated the waiting bottle of brandy. Juan and Isabel, who had rushed in from the street, tried to find out, without their mother noticing what they were doing, if he'd brought them any presents.

It was a quarter of an hour later, when she was in the kitchen, that Dolores called out: 'Are you there, Enrique?' She came and stood in the doorway, a wooden spoon in one hand. 'Go and ring Cousin Francisca and tell her you're back safely.'

'Why?'

'Because that's what she asked me to ask you to do.' She turned and disappeared from sight.

'Hurry up and get your feet right under the table,' said Jaime, a salacious grin on his face.

Alvarez drained his glass, refilled it, carried it through to the front room. He dialled the number. 'Cousin Francisca, it's Enrique.'

'So you have survived! I'm so glad. Cousin Dolores has buried you several times.'

'She does worry, doesn't she?'

'Quite naturally. I suppose you realize you ruined my little family party by going away when you did?'

'I'm terribly sorry, but there was just nothing I could do about it.'

'Of course there wasn't; I was only teasing. Cousin Dolores said you should have refused to leave until Monday, but as I told her, you just couldn't do that . . . I suppose she's told you what's happening?'

'She hasn't told me anything yet.'

'Well, because I wanted to entertain all the family together, we agreed to put everything off for a week. I had a word with the butcher who said that it would be quite all right to keep the meat in the fridge for a week, so that's what I've done. The party's next Sunday. I do hope that on Saturday you won't ring to say you're suddenly flying off to South Africa.'

'There's no chance of that.'

'Then I'll see you all on Sunday.'

He said goodbye and returned to the dining-room.

'Well?' asked Jaime.

'I just told her I was back.'

'And?'

'And she said we were all eating there next Sunday.'

'As soon as she heard you weren't going to be here last Sunday, it was wait until you are. Shows where you stand, doesn't it? You won't know yourself in a big house with all that land. You're a lucky old goat!'

Armitage was backing out of a slot in the hotel car park when Alvarez drove in and alongside. 'You want me?' he asked aggressively, as he thrust his head through the open window and the sun raised lights in his beard.

'I would like a word with you, yes, señor.'

'Is that a request or an order?'

'I prefer to call it a request.'

'As polite as bloody ever. Do you reckon you'll arrest me politely?'

'I shall not be arresting you.'

Armitage moistened his lips with his tongue. 'No?'

'You did not murder either Pedro or Señor Gaspari.'

'I know that, but do you?'

'I'm afraid it's taken a long time to be certain, señor, because I have been unable to see sufficiently clearly. I felt certain you were innocent, even when a glass in Señor Gaspari's house, used on the night of his murder, proved to have your fingerprints on it . . .'

'Jesus! What's been going on?'

'A clever man has been trying to escape the past.'

Armitage stared across for several seconds, then said abruptly: 'I need a bloody strong drink.'

Five minutes later, they were in Armitage's bedroom. He opened the cupboard and brought out bottle, glasses and vacuum flask, carried these across to the table. 'All right. Are you going to tell me precisely what's been going on?'

'That depends on whether you're a vindictive man?'

'I'll tell you something. I pride myself on being able to understand the real person behind the face, but every time I think I've got you lined up, you do or say something that throws me. Am I vindictive? What the hell's it matter whether I am?'

'Because I need to know if you will search for happiness or revenge.'

He poured out the drinks, handed a glass to Alvarez, crossed to the window and stared out to sea. 'Then you're certain my father was murdered?'

'Yes, I am.'

Armitage drained his glass, returned to the table and poured himself a second drink. 'If it was a month ago, I'd be shouting for revenge. I've a quick temper. But it happened almost fifty years ago. Time softens everything; history touches the intellect, not the emotions. Then, I'd be revenging myself on a murderer; now, who would I be facing? Fifty years change a man so much, both physically and mentally, that he's a different person.'

'Then you choose happiness? Seize it, señor, before it has time to run away from you. And remember, distance can ease sorrow nearly as much as does time. So persuade the señora to leave the island with you and find your happiness together.'

'I suppose you realize that I don't know what in the goddamn hell you're really talking about?'

'Perhaps not now, but before long I am afraid that you will.'

The third week of July brought even greater heat and during the day it almost seemed as if the air might at any time catch fire. Alvarez parked by the side of the lean-to garage and by the time he reached the front door, where Scalfaro was waiting, he was sweating profusely. 'Good morning,' he said, as he used a handkerchief to wipe his forehead and face. 'The señora is here still?'

'No.'

'She has left the island?'

'Does that concern you?'

'Very much.'

Scalfaro, angry and a shade uncertain, said: 'Damned if I can see why . . . I suppose you want a drink?' He stepped out of the doorway and led the way round the house to a tiled patio at the side.

Alvarez sat, in the shade; Scalfaro went indoors through the back door. He returned with a tray on which was a bottle, two glasses and an ice bucket. Silent, he poured out drinks, passed one glass across.

'Has the señora left the island?' Alvarez asked for the second time.

'Yes.'

'With Señor Armitage?'

'Just what's the point of these questions?'

'I want to find out if she will have the support of a good man to help her through troubled times.'

'A good man?' Scalfaro's tone was ironic. 'My impression was that you considered Steven anything but that.'

'I can be more certain of the truth since I have visited Italy.'

'Really?' He managed to sound bored.

'When I was there, I spoke to two people who knew Count Capria very well and they were able to tell me what kind of a man he was.'

'And that is so important?'

'Yes, because it also tells me what kind of a man he is not. He is not a morose man, who shuns company, is socially uneasy in many situations, and has such little taste that he collects pornography and reads only the poorest fiction. In fact, he was not Señor Gaspari. You are Count Alfredo Capria.'

Scalfaro laughed.

'During the war you were transferred to naval Intelligence, a transfer you found much to your liking since the new job exercised some of your natural talents. After a while you were put in charge of the secret submarine base in Puerto Llueso.

'The existence of the base was not quite the secret everyone on your side believed and an English naval officer, Perry Armitage, was detailed clandestinely—because Spain was a neutral country whom the Allies had at all costs to avoid upsetting—to find out as much about it as he could. Sadly, he took too great a risk and was exposed as a spy.

'Your natural talents are those of a sadist; you enjoy inflicting mental and physical pain. You used both in order to try to force Señor Armitage to divulge how much he'd discovered and passed on to the British. Due to his bravery and your negligent over-enthusiasm, you killed him before he told you anything. The loss of three, perhaps four, submarines after they left Llueso Bay marked his victory over you.

'You'd shown you were a far-seeing man when you moved most of your fortune out of Italy before the war started. You proved that again after Perry Armitage died. You could foresee that the Allies would win and call to account all those who had been guilty of war crimes. An intelligent man always accepts that fate may run against him, so you decided to "die", thereby bringing to an abrupt end any investigation into your exploits that might be begun. It would be a very cleverly faked death, yet even so there had to be the further possibility that evidence of such fakery might come to light through an unforeseeable sequence of events. So you decided not only to change names after "dying", but to change identities before you "died". And you could be certain that the Spanish authorities, as able as you to see the course the war must now take, would be willing accomplices.

'You met Filippo Nicolazzi at the rest camp. I imagine that his life story which you presented to me as yours was true to some essentials, but false in others—you embellished because you had to explain how you, if from so unpromising a background, could possess the social ease of someone from a privileged one. Nicolazzi suited you, despite a complete lack of social polish, because he had no known relatives, no possessions, and nothing to look forward to after the war. You had him assigned to your group. Later, here, when you were about to change identities, you engaged his ignorant acquiescence in your plans by offering him a standard of life far superior to that which he could ever otherwise hope to enjoy. The Spanish authorities—very high authorities— accepted him as Count Alfredo Capria whose name they agreed should be changed to Giovanni Gaspari. He was your insurance.

'Your capital was in a safe bolt-hole—probably Switzer-land. Had you drawn on this directly, this would have opened a lead which could expose you, despite the strict banking laws in that country. So you used the Franziskaner Bank in Liechtenstein as a postbox, not to hide the capital deeper, but to hide the fact that the income was yours. Every week a sum of money from your Swiss bank was paid into an account in the name of Gaspari in the Liechtenstein bank. Then he drew cheques in his name and paid you the larger proportion of the money. Obviously, he was never able to touch your capital or to draw more in total than you decided. And because he gave you money, it would have to appear that you were dependent on him; if you were dependent on him, clearly he had to be the Count . . .

'Through a set of circumstances which not even you, as clever as you are, could have foreseen, Steven Armitage came to the island to search for the truth about his father's death—a truth that had deliberately been obscured by the British authorities, a bonus which I doubt you knew about. When he made contact with Pedro, he was getting a little too close to the truth for you to stand by and do nothing, so, ever clever, you had Pedro murdered under the guise of accidental death.

'Events didn't proceed as you'd planned because you'd overlooked the one thing that so many criminals have dis-covered to their cost—the very act of concealing, reveals. The more I learned, the more potentially dangerous I became, to the point where you tried to have me assassi-nated. Thankfully, that attempt failed. Because it did, you had to cash in your insurance—you murdered Señor Gaspari so that Count Capria should die a second and final time.'

'Ingenious, amusing, but fiction from beginning to end.'

'Are you really so confident that I can't prove you to be Count Capria? That's not being quite so clever, is it? The two people in Italy I spoke to were your wife and your cousin; despite what the years have done to you, they must surely be able to identify you. When you deposited your fortune before the war, you must have had to identify yourself. With the permission of the bank—and this is a criminal case—that identification can be followed through. Or are you really asking me if it can be proved that you have murdered three times? After all, officially Lieutenant Armitage died in France and both the British and the Spanish authorities would prefer that version of events to hold, so that one can expect virtually no help from them in unravelling the truth of his death; Pedro's death still cannot be shown beyond question to have been deliberate and not accidental and perhaps never will be; what little evidence exists in Señor Gaspari's murder points to Señor Armitage as the murderer, not you.'

'Then it would seem that your version of events must remain fiction. You can't arrest me.'

'Oh, but I can.'

'If you haven't any proof—'

'For bigamy.'

'What?' Scalfaro was bewildered.

'When you married on this island, your wife in Italy still lived.'

'I married here as Scalfaro.'

'You think any court would listen to so absurd a defence?'

'I know people in very high positions; they'll see no case ever comes to court.'

'They might well prevent any further action regarding the death of Lieutenant Armitage, on the grounds of national interest. But bigamy is a sordid, small-minded betrayal of moral and religious decency and no democratic government would dare run the risk of being caught trying to protect a man guilty of such a crime.'

There was a long silence. Scalfaro drained his glass, put it down on the table. 'Forget all you've just told me and I'll make it very well worth your while. You can retire, buy yourself a really nice house . . .'

'Do you think that because you could so easily seduce

Señor Gaspari with money, you can do the same to everyone else?'

'Your conscience is worth more than a fortune?'

'I hope so.'

'Then you're a fool.'

'That is almost certainly so. After all, I was very distressed when I considered how your daughter must suffer when she learned the truth about you and her illegitimacy and I considered appealing to you to try and spare her pain. Only then did I realize that a man who will set out falsely to name his daughter's lover a murderer is hardly likely to be concerned about her feelings . . . But even a fool can have a flash of wisdom and I decided that the only way of persuading you to do something was to show that it will affect you in some beneficial way . . .

'There must have been many times when you have thought with pride that in Italy Count Capria is remembered as a young, highly decorated naval officer who died for his country. All those contemporaries, from families with ancient and noble lineages, who had so often looked down on you before the war—they could not hold a war hero in contempt. Your wife, whom you had married for her background, who had learned to hate you—she could not wholly despise a war hero. Your cousin, Señor Darida, whose mother had made the mistake of marrying for love, not money, had loathed you, but he had to remember you as a war hero. How are these people now going to think of Count Alfredo Capria, convicted bigamist? They will think of him with satisfied contempt.'

'Why . . .'

'There is more for you to consider. Men in high places will be very, very quick to disown a bigamist. Once you are without their protection, you become very vulnerable where the recent murders are concerned. Nothing can be done without leaving traces of the doing, and so sooner or later the proof will be gathered that it was you who murdered Señor Gaspari, that it was you who murdered, or had murdered, Pedro the Simple, that it was you who tried to have me murdered. Then you will become a bigamist also convicted of murder. Twice despicable, ten times more despised.'

'In God's name, man, why don't you listen to what I'm offering you?'

'Perhaps it would be more rewarding for you to listen to me. There is still one thing you can do to save what's most precious to you—your reputation in the memories of others.' Alvarez stood. 'I wonder if you have the courage to do it. If not, I shall arrest you for bigamy tomorrow.'

Alvarez received the telephone message at 9.30 that night.

'Señor Scalfaro has been found dead. It seems he shot himself.'

He thanked the caller, replaced the receiver. As he stared through the unshuttered window at the street, he wondered to what extent others might hold him accountable for events for which he felt no guilt; he hoped that Armitage's love would soften Nicola's grief.

CHAPTER 24

'What on earth are you doing up there?' Dolores shouted in tones of exasperation.

'Changing my shirt,' Alvarez called back.

'Get a move on. We're late already.'

He slipped the shirt over his head. If she'd wanted to arrive dead on one, she should not have criticized the shirt he had been wearing and demanded he change into a clean one.

When he returned downstairs, everyone was waiting in the front room. Dolores studied him closely and evidently he passed muster this time because she said: 'Come on. Cousin Francisca likes people to be on time.'

'Why?' asked Juan.

'If you've nothing sensible to say, keep you mouth shut. Isabel, stop scuffing your shoes.'

'I wasn't,' she replied.

'Don't argue with me, young lady, or you'll be in considerable trouble. Jaime, are you just standing there because you've lost what few wits you once had?'

'What's got you so sharp?'

'Because I have to deal with a family who seem incapable of doing anything correctly.'

They were silent for most of the drive; experience had taught them that when Dolores was in one of her moods, silence was not only golden, it was also safe.

The gates were open and Alvarez was able to turn directly on to the dirt track up to Ca'n Pyloto. Bathed in brilliant sunshine, the mountains on the far side of the valley provided a dramatic, yet for once unforeboding, backdrop.

'Jaime,' Dolores snapped, 'I don't want to hear any of your jokes. I'm not having Cousin Francisca thinking we're a crude family. Enrique, no matter what the meal's like, you're to say it's delicious.'

Alvarez braked the car to a halt. 'I'll even tell her she's a better cook than you.'

Jaime laughed, which showed he was not a very wise man.

Francisca met them at the front door. She kissed each of the adults on both cheeks, gave Isabel a hug and went to do the same to Juan, but he carefully evaded her, much to the anger of his mother. She stepped back. 'Well, Enrique, so you've managed to make it this time!'

'The superior chief wanted me to go to Canada today, but I said I'd something much more important to do.'

She smiled. 'Come along in. I do hope the meal's all right. I did exactly as you suggested, Dolores, and the last time I pecked the crackling was looking just right . . . You're a spoilt man, Enrique, living with such a wonderful cook. It makes me very nervous.'

'I'm certain you've no need to be.'

They went into the formal sitting-room. Once they were seated, Francisca said: 'I'll just have to leave you for a moment.' She hurried out of the room.

Jaime turned to his right, then to his left. His expression became worried.

'What's the matter?' Dolores demanded.

'Just looking.'

'What for?'

'Just looking,' he repeated in a mumble.

There was a short silence, broken by Juan. 'I want to go.'

'I told you to before we came,' said Dolores.

'I did.'

'Then you can't possibly want to go again.'

'But I do.'

She said something under her breath. 'It's through that doorway and then on your left.' She was silent until Juan had left, then she said: 'It's a lovely house.' No one commented. 'Isn't it?' she snapped, staring hard at Alvarez.

'Yes.'

'Is that all you've got to say?'

'What more do you want me . . .'

'Nothing,' she interrupted forcefully.

Juan and Francisca returned at the same moment, entering through different doors. She said: 'Everything's ready, so we can go through. Enrique, would you like to give me a hand to get the meat out of the oven? It's rather heavy and if I've a strong man in the house, I don't see why I shouldn't make use of him!'

As the rest of the family went through to the dining-room, Alvarez followed her into the kitchen. She handed him an oven cloth and he used this to take the baking tray out of the oven and to put it on a board. After lifting the lechona on to a dish, he carried it through to the dining-room.

Francisca followed him. 'Enrique, would you like to carve? It's a job I do so hate doing.' She smiled. 'It really is useful having a man in the house!'

'And satisfying,' said Jaime. He winced, as Dolores kicked him.

'Maybe,' said Francisca to Jaime, 'you'd serve the drinks while Enrique is carving?'

'Of course.' He pushed back his chair and stood, looked round for the wine.

'There's orangeade and lemonade keeping cold in the fridge; and there's also water in a plastic bottle for anyone who prefers that.' She noticed his expression. 'I'm afraid there's nothing stronger. Since my poor husband died, I won't have alcohol in the house.'

Strangely, when Dolores was really angry, she usually became silent, in sharp contrast to those occasions when she was merely annoyed and had no hesitation in making others fully aware of that fact. But finally, as they reached the end of the valley to come in sight of Llueso, she said furiously: 'How could you have behaved so badly?'

No one answered.

'Why wouldn't you even talk to her, Enrique?'

Alvarez concentrated still harder on his driving.

'I've never been so ashamed! I could have wept. After all I've done for you, you behaved like a peasant from Mestara! Have you no sense of gratitude?'

'You kept warning her I was impossible, so she can't have been very surprised,' said Alvarez, finally stung into defending his behaviour.

'What is that supposed to mean?'

'You told me often enough how you've made excuses for my crude behaviour.'

'I've never said anything of the sort to her. I said it to you because I didn't want you to understand that she'd make you the perfect wife. If I'd told you she would, because you're so perverse and pig-headed, you'd have had nothing more to do with her.' She drew in a deep breath. 'Men!' she suddenly shouted, causing Alvarez to start so heavily that the car swerved and nearly hit an oncoming van.

They arrived home. Alvarez and Jaime climbed out of the car and tilted their seats forward to allow those in the back to get out. They stared at each other across the roof and there was no need for words. As soon as it was safe, they'd head for the nearest bar.